His eyes darted aw
before returning to

"That's great, what you'

Nodding, Lucy knew when not to push. "Well, we're here every Monday. If you change your mind, you're welcome to come back."

She turned to go, and dropped her head as the rain started to pick up intensity.

"I lost my wife six months ago."

His low tone was nearly drowned out by the rain, but Lucy froze, knowing full well she'd heard correctly. Shoving her damp hair off her forehead, she turned back around.

"My husband has been gone for two years," she replied, wanting him to know they already had something in common and he wasn't alone. Still, saying the words never got any easier; it was just an ugly fact she'd learned to live with. "I'm available to talk one-on-one, too, if you prefer."

He stared at her a bit longer as if he was trying to process what move to make next. That internal struggle was real, and it was something he had to battle himself. She waited for his reply, not caring how wet she was getting, how her hair was clinging to her cheeks or her shirt had plastered itself to her skin.

With a tip of his hat, he nodded toward the church. "You'd best get inside. Storm's comin'."

RETURN TO STONEROCK:
In this small Tennessee town,
neighbors find the warmth of home...and love.

Dear Reader,

I'm so pleased to return to Stonerock, Tennessee! Thank you for coming along on this journey with me. If you read my original series, The St. Johns of Stonerock, you'll recognize some returning characters.

But let's start with Lucy and Noah. This hero and heroine have been speaking to me for years now, and I am finally letting them have their moment. A single widower with an adorable little girl, and a woman who's lost so much yet refuses to let life knock her down. Who doesn't want to cheer for these two and their much-deserved happily-ever-after?

Small-town romances have always held a special place in my heart...perhaps because I live in a small town of my own and married my high school sweetheart. There's nothing greater than seeing two hearts heal each other, though, and Lucy and Noah are overdue for some happiness in their lives.

I hope you all are ready for some laughter and tears because these two will run you through all the emotions as they struggle to find their way through the pain and into each other's hearts.

And don't worry, there will be even more fascinating characters that come through Stonerock. I can't wait to introduce them all to you!

Happy reading,

Jules

The Cowboy's Second-Chance Family

Jules Bennett

HARLEQUIN® SPECIAL EDITION®

Recycling programs
for this product may
not exist in your area.

ISBN-13: 978-0-373-62371-6

The Cowboy's Second-Chance Family

Copyright © 2017 by Jules Bennett

Printed in U.S.A.

National bestselling author **Jules Bennett** has penned over forty contemporary romance novels. She lives in the Midwest with her high-school-sweetheart husband and their two kids. Jules can often be found on Twitter chatting with readers, and you can also connect with her via her website, julesbennett.com.

Books by Jules Bennett

Harlequin Special Edition

The St. Johns of Stonerock

Dr. Daddy's Perfect Christmas
The Fireman's Ready-Made Family
From Best Friend to Bride

Harlequin Desire

What the Prince Wants
A Royal Amnesia Scandal
Maid for a Magnate
His Secret Baby Bombshell

Mafia Moguls

Trapped with the Tycoon
From Friend to Fake Fiancé
Holiday Baby Scandal
The Heir's Unexpected Baby

The Rancher's Heirs

Twin Secrets
Claimed by the Rancher

Visit her Author Profile page at Harlequin.com, or julesbennett.com, for more titles.

To all the readers who requested more books
set in Stonerock: here you go!
I also threw in a cowboy. You're welcome :)

Chapter One

The mysterious man sitting in the back of the room didn't want to be seen. Too bad, because Lucy Brooks had spotted him the second he'd tried to slip in unnoticed twenty minutes ago.

A sexy man with broad shoulders, perfectly tanned skin, denim worn out in all the proper places, and clutching a black cowboy hat could not simply blend in. That square, stubbled jaw alone would grab any woman's attention. Not that Lucy wanted to be grabbed.

She tried to focus as one of the regular attendees discussed her one positive experience from the past week. The Helping Hands support group Lucy had started with her best friends Tara and Kate was a way to encourage others struggling with grief. Everyone brought something different to the meetings because everyone handled the loss of a loved one differently. And nobody had the same story to tell.

Which brought her gaze back to the cowboy in the back. Stonerock, Tennessee, had its fair share of ranchers, but she'd never seen this man before. The fact he was new explained the jumbled nerves in her belly. She refused to believe they were caused by the dark stare he was returning in her direction.

"Does anyone else have anything they'd like to share?" Tara asked, pulling Lucy back to the moment. When nobody stepped forward, Tara went on. "Remember, we will be changing the starting time next week. We'll be switching to seven instead of six. Have a great week, everybody."

All in attendance tonight were regulars, save for the cowboy. They'd all had a positive week and tonight's meeting had mostly been smiles and laughter—the whole reason for forming this group nearly two years ago.

Lucy excused herself from her friends and headed toward the back of the church where the new guy was trying to sneak out as quickly and quietly as he'd snuck in.

Lucy wasn't having any part of that. She made her way through the aisles, smiling and nodding to familiar faces. But when she reached the back, the stranger was gone. Jogging out the open doors, she spotted him striding toward a big black truck. What else would a mysterious cowboy drive?

A fine mist covered her face as she picked up the pace to catch up with him. Those long legs of his ate up some serious ground.

He must've heard or sensed her because he glanced over his shoulder and stopped. Swiping the dampness from her face, Lucy finished closing the gap between them.

"Hi. I'm Lucy." Okay, that sounded lame, but she didn't know what else to lead with. She was usually fine with greeting new guests, but this man was different. "I wanted to welcome you to the group, but you slipped out before I could say hello."

The stranger shoved his black hat back on and fished the keys from his pocket. "I'm not joining. Just wanted to come by and see what it was about."

She recognized that emptiness she saw in his dark eyes, knew that denial, that unspoken insistence he'd be all right without help. Even with the light rain and only the glow from the church lights, she had become all too familiar with that look. Two years ago she'd seen it every day staring back at her in the mirror.

"You've lost someone recently?" When his jaw clenched, she knew she'd hit the mark. He was the angry griever. There were all types and she'd come to know them all. "Would you like to come back in and talk?"

The stranger snorted and shook his head as he

turned toward his truck and held out his key fob. Lights flashed as the locks were released.

"No, I wouldn't. I'm not baring my soul to a group of strangers."

Lucy wrapped her arms around her waist. Occasionally rude people came through, but she'd had to remind herself the words weren't necessarily directed at her. They were targeted toward the person's inner anger.

The stranger cursed on a sigh and turned back to her. "Noah. My name is Noah."

Lucy smiled. Apparently his guilt trumped his anger where she was concerned. A cowboy *and* a gentleman.

"I didn't plan on making you bare your soul, just so you know. I didn't know if you'd like to come in and just talk, not necessarily about loss or grieving. We actually get together once a week and discuss a variety of things."

One thick, dark brow quirked. "Like what?"

Lucy shrugged. "One rule is if you're going to speak, you have to start with something good that happened since you were here last. It can be anything. We are really just here to lift each other up, not focus on why we're hurting."

His eyes darted away for a brief second before returning to her. "That's great, what you're doing. It's just…not for me."

Nodding, Lucy knew when not to push. "Well,

we're here every Monday. If you change your mind, you're welcome to come back."

When she turned to go, she dropped her head as the rain started to pick up intensity.

"I lost my wife six months ago."

His low tone was nearly drowned out by the rain, but Lucy froze, knowing full well she'd heard correctly. Shoving her damp hair off her forehead, she turned back around.

"My husband has been gone for two years," she replied, wanting him to know they already had something in common and he wasn't alone. Still, saying the words never got any easier. It was just an ugly fact she'd learned to live with. "I'm available to talk one-on-one, too, if you prefer."

He stared at her a bit longer, as if he was trying to process what move to make next. That internal struggle was real, but something he had to battle himself. She waited for his reply, not caring how wet she was getting, how her hair was clinging to her cheeks or how her shirt had plastered itself to her skin.

With a tip of his hat, he nodded toward the church. "You'd best get inside. Storm's comin'."

Gripping the steering wheel until his knuckles turned white, Noah Spencer headed home. Well, to the house he was renting. Calling the place he'd lived in only a few days a home was quite a stretch.

He'd lost his ranch, a portion of his life that he'd never get back. Noah swallowed as guilt and grief threatened to overtake him. The loss of his wife was far greater than that of the land and livestock. But losing nearly everything all at once was damn near soul-crushing.

Settling into this small town, ready to start his new job with the Stonerock Police Department tomorrow night, was the fresh start he needed. Being a rancher was his first love, but the failing ranch he'd had in Texas was gone and the money to rebuild simply wasn't there.

If he were all alone he would've tried to come up with a way to fight for that dream…or close himself off from the world and curse fate for taking so much from him.

But he hadn't quite lost everything and he wasn't alone. He had a little girl depending on him to provide security, a stable home, and the vision of a brighter future.

Noah smiled despite the pain. Just the thought of Emma, his girly-girl with her pink bows and her curly blond hair, always brightened his mood. She'd dealt with this move far better than he had. To her, everything in life was an adventure and he'd do well to learn from her positive outlook.

And it was that positive attitude of Emma's that drove him to check out this support group he'd heard of. When his real estate agent had lined up this rental until he could find a house worth buying in his budget, she'd mentioned various things around town: a few trustworthy babysitters, good restaurants, pediatricians…and this group. Helping Hands was free to the community, to help lift up people who had lost someone.

Noah truly didn't care about being lifted up or any other mind tricks meant to make him feel better about his life. Right now it sucked. Plain and simple. There was no way to sugarcoat things and he was too mentally exhausted to try.

Forcing the bitterness away, he pulled into his drive. For the sake of his daughter, he always put up a strong front. That was his job as her sole parent now. She mourned the loss of her mother, of her pets back at the leveled ranch, so he needed to always keep her surroundings positive.

Killing the engine, Noah sat there and thought back to the blonde beauty who'd followed him out to his truck. She'd been determined to get him to open up and he'd been just as determined not to. Yet something about her sweet smile, those piercing green eyes, and her soft tone had made him reveal more than he'd wanted to.

Her opening up about her late husband had surprised him. Even through the sadness in her tone, she'd smiled. For him. A total stranger reaching out to him. She'd invited him back, but…

Noah sighed and jerked his door handle. He wasn't

going back. Attending meetings like that would only make him relive the nightmare of six months ago. He'd moved to Stonerock for a fresh start and that's exactly what he planned on getting. How could he move forward if he was constantly reminded about how drastically his life had changed?

Heading up the walkway, Noah glanced toward the bay window where his whole reason for living was waving wildly. Curls bouncing, plastic tiara askew, Emma made a silly face. Noah couldn't help but laugh as he reflected one back to her. He knew the second he walked through that door and relieved the baby-sitter that he'd be trading his cowboy hat for a tiara and Emma would pull out her makeup so they could play dress-up.

There was nowhere else in the world he'd rather be. He didn't need a support group to help him move on; he only needed his four-year-old princess.

Yet the blonde and her open invitation stayed in the forefront of his mind and he refused to even ac-knowledge the knot in his gut when he thought of how striking she was, how patient and how compassionate. And he sure as hell needed to forget how her wet shirt had plastered itself to her curves, punching him full-on with the first taste of attraction he'd had since—

No. He refused to even go there right now. All he needed was his daughter, his job and this new beginning. No way in hell was he adding a woman to that list.

* * *

Taking a deep breath, Noah stepped inside the Stonerock Police Department and was hit with the scent of burned coffee. Good thing he'd already had two cups before he left his house. He wasn't used to working the midnight shift back in Texas, but he was the low man on the totem pole at this station, and he needed the job.

He'd always loved the mountains of Tennessee; he and his wife had honeymooned there. When he'd wanted to get away from Texas, he'd immediately thought of Tennessee. It didn't take long to narrow his search down to other departments that were seeking another officer.

A bulletin board hung immediately to his left, full of images of missing persons and various announcements from other authorities, local and national. A couple of old scarred desks filled with folders and papers, but no one manning them, were to his right. He'd been here only twice before for interviews and to turn in paperwork, but he knew the town was low on crime and the office usually only had a handful of staff at a time.

Noah moved through the department and headed toward the captain's office. Cameron St. John was one hell of a captain, and rumor had it he'd put a stop to drug runners threatening this humble town only a year ago. While Noah may long to be back on the ranch, no matter how rough finances had been, he was also anxious and excited to be working for such a well-respected department.

"That's because you always burn the coffee. If you'd let me make it, at least we could drink it without choking on it."

Noah froze. That feminine voice washed over him, instantly taking him back to the parking lot the night before, to the silky tone from the blonde with rain dampening her face. She'd talked to him as if she weren't getting soaked, as if she didn't look like she'd stepped from a wet T-shirt contest. Her only concern had been for him…which said quite a bit about her character.

Noah gritted his teeth and forced those wet T-shirt images aside. Before he could take a step forward, Lucy stepped from the captain's office and smacked right into him. Instinct had him reaching up to grip her arms—toned yet delicate arms. She was a petite little thing, the top of her head hitting below his chin.

Noah dropped his hands, but her palms were flat against his chest. The second she tipped her head back and her eyes focused on his face, she raised her brows in surprise.

Lucy took a step back. "You're the new officer?" she gasped, then shook her head. "Clearly you are. I mean, you're in uniform. I just…"

She trailed off as pink tinged her cheeks, and something about having her flustered when she'd been in such control last night had him fighting back a grin. Other than Emma, nobody had made him grin in a long, long time.

He took in her buttoned-up white sweater and dark jeans. She had some sparkly earrings that his daughter would covet on sight and deem princess material.

"I didn't see you when I came in before." Damn it, why had he said that?

"I'm a part-time night dispatcher," she explained, tucking her hair behind her ear. "I'm finishing up my online master's classes and it eats up most of my time."

And she also ran a free outreach program for the community. Clearly she stayed busy, which was exactly what he needed to do. Ogling his new coworker was not the hobby he needed to look into.

Noah gestured behind her toward the open door. "If you'll excuse me, I need to check in."

Lucy blinked, then stepped aside. "Sorry, I didn't mean to hold you up. I'm just surprised to see you again. I mean…"

"Yeah," he agreed, not wanting to discuss last night.

He'd had a moment of weakness, but his head was on straight now and he was moving forward, starting with this new position. No way in hell would he be seen as vulnerable. What type of cop would that make him? His duties included being strong, fierce, in control—none of which he felt one hundred percent about. But he had to start somewhere and rehashing last night wasn't the place.

"I'm sure I'll see you later. I better go fix that coffee."

With a smile, Lucy headed down the hallway and Noah cursed himself for watching her go. This beautiful woman who'd caught him at a fragile moment could not interfere with his goal of building a new life for his daughter.

Chapter Two

Lucy cursed her shaky hands. She knew the rookie officer was coming on board tonight, but she'd had no idea the mysterious man she'd met last night would be one and the same.

She wasn't sure if he looked better in a Stetson and jeans or the navy blue uniform, but she wouldn't turn away a chance at looking at both. Looking was harmless, right? Mercy, but he did get her heart rate up and there wasn't a doubt in her mind that once the single ladies of Stonerock realized there was a new officer, they'd be all over him. Parking tickets could quite possibly multiply in the foreseeable future.

The glorious aroma of freshly brewed coffee filled

the tiny break room, masking the burned odor that had pervaded previously. She didn't know how this crew got along without her on her nights off. Soon she'd have her degree in psychology and she could find a job counseling military wives and families.

"Lucy."

She jerked around, startled at the gruff tone of Officer McCoy. He was a giant teddy bear, older and a little pudgy in the midsection, but an amazing cop.

"Hey." She greeted him with a smile. "I didn't hear you come in."

"I need you to spend a few hours with Officer Spencer. Carla was going to, but she had to leave suddenly to get to the nursing home for her mom and there's a last-minute meeting so he's getting paired with you for just a bit."

Perfect. Spending some up close and personal time with the town's newest officer would be fine… if she weren't a bundle of nerves just looking at the man.

All she knew was that he was a widower; she'd learned that last night after the meeting. Word around the station was that he was from a small town outside of Houston, Texas. That was pretty much the extent of what she knew of Noah Spencer.

Well, that wasn't entirely true. She knew he had a swagger that could make a woman's knees go weak and he had that Southern drawl that had her belly curling with arousal.

Still, she shouldn't be eyeing the new guy with such affection, or any coworker for that matter. The town was small and everyone in this department was like one big, happy family.

"No problem," she stated, lying through her teeth. "I'm happy to help out." That part was true; she'd pinch hit for her fellow dispatchers whenever she was needed. "I just had to get this coffee going since Officer James burned the last pot."

"James tries hard, but she's never made a decent pot in her life," McCoy grumbled. "Thanks for saving us. James just went out on a domestic dispute, by the way. She's better on the streets than in this break room."

Lucy laughed as she turned to reach for a mug from the counter. "At least she tries. Let me get a cup and I'll be right out to talk to Officer Spencer."

First she needed some caffeine because this was going to be a long night. A dose of coffee to add to her jitters. Perfect.

But she was a professional and so was Noah. Besides, he hadn't shown the slightest interest, so this little infatuation was quite possibly one-sided. The man was still mourning his wife for pity's sake. She could appreciate his looks and perhaps this learning period would get him to open up. He didn't have to come to meetings to heal.

She poured her cup of coffee and just as she turned, she ran into a solid chest. The hot liquid spilled onto her hand, burning her skin and causing her to drop the mug, which then hit the floor and shattered.

Firm hands gripped her shoulders. "You all right?"

Noah's worried look had her nodding, though her hand burned. "Did I spill coffee all over you?"

Great first impression, Lucy. Way to get him to notice you.

"How's your hand?" he asked, ignoring her question as he took her wet hand in his. "Did you burn yourself?"

"It's fine." Could she be more of a fool? "Let me get something to clean off your shoes. Are you sure it's not on your uniform?"

Thankfully the uniform was navy blue, but still, she didn't want to have him soaking wet and smelling like he was a barista on patrol.

Still holding on to her hand, Noah led her to the sink and turned on the cold water. "This is looking a little red."

Was it? Because the way he was holding on to her and the way his body aligned with hers, she really had no clue anything else existed except him.

"You okay?"

Lucy glanced over her shoulder at Officer McCoy, who stood in the doorway. "Just dropped my coffee," she replied.

"I'll clean it up."

He disappeared for a moment and came back with

the mop. As he started cleaning, Lucy realized Noah was still holding her hand under the water. She focused her attention on him and smiled.

"I'm fine. Really."

Noah's dark eyes seemed so dull, so…sad. She wanted to reach out to him, somehow. Nobody should live in misery. Wasn't that the whole reason she and her friends had started the group? They were each recovering and wanted to get others to live again.

Noah turned the water off and reached for a paper towel. When he started to wrap her hand, she took the towel from him and did it herself. Too much touching was dangerous…at least to her mental state. She was to work with him, and hopefully get him to open up and recover from his loss, so anything beyond that wasn't an option.

Besides, she'd vowed never to fall for a man who risked his life on a daily basis ever again. Living through hell once was more than enough for her.

"I can get that," she said as she turned her attention to McCoy.

"You made the coffee, that's enough." He picked up the large jagged mug pieces and tossed them in the trash before soaking up the liquid. "Get to work and make sure you don't pull any pranks on Spencer here."

She glanced to Noah, who was still standing far closer and smelling far better than should be legal.

"I'll have you know that last stunt with the sugar and salt with the coffee was not me. It was Carla."

When he grunted, Lucy merely glanced to Noah and shrugged. She headed from the break room, well aware the new officer was directly behind her. If only Carla were here tonight to help take some of this pressure from Lucy. She'd never had this instant attraction before so she seriously needed to get ahold of herself.

Why did the first interest since her husband's death have to be a man dealing with such grief? He was in no place to even look her way, let alone flirt.

Flirt? Mercy sakes, what was she saying? They had a job to do and she'd do well to remember they were technically coworkers.

"Are you sure your hand is okay?" he asked as they came to the dispatch desks with all of the monitors and phones.

"It's fine." How many times could she say fine? "Did you get cleaned up?"

He glanced to his shiny, patent leather shoes. "They just got splashed. I think your hand and the floor took everything."

When he looked back up, his eyes went straight to her chest. Well, maybe this attraction wasn't one-sided.

"You have coffee on your sweater."

And perhaps it was, because he wasn't looking at her boobs at all, but the coffee she'd spilled. She knew her sweater was damp, but she didn't exactly have another shirt to put on. And of course it was a white sweater. Classy. So classy.

"It will dry," she stated, waving a hand through the air as if she wasn't bothered, though she was cringing each time his eyes dropped to the stain.

She took a seat at her desk and gestured to the empty chair beside her. "How long have you been in Stonerock?"

"Almost a week."

Lucy pointed to one of the monitors with the layout of the town. "I assume you've been out driving around and familiarizing yourself with the area."

He nodded. "The streets are a grid. Pretty easy to get around."

"This won't be much different from where you were before," she explained. "Stonerock is small, low crime. I'm sure you know all of that, but you will get to know the people in no time."

As she explained how things would work from her end, he nodded and listened without interruption. When the line lit up, Lucy held up her hand and took the call.

The frantic voice of a child came over the headset and Lucy went into that calm mode she had to settle into when trying to offer comfort to the stranger on the other end. And when that stranger happened to be a child, Lucy tried to compartmentalize her feelings and remain in control.

"My mommy is having a baby," the little boy screamed. "Right now!" The child's voice was drowned out by a woman's cries.

Lucy went to the flip cards on the desk and found the one she needed to issue the proper orders. This wasn't her first baby call and it wouldn't be her last. She managed to get a neighbor's name and called her while keeping the child on the line. While paramedics were on their way, Lucy wanted another adult there for the child.

All in all, the call took about four minutes before the medical squad arrived on the scene and the neighbor came to take the little boy. Lucy disconnected the call once everyone was safe and taken care of.

As she eased back in her seat, she caught a side glance of Noah. The adrenaline during the call had her completely forgetting about him—and that was saying something.

"You did good," he commented.

Lucy laughed. "Well, that's my job, so…"

"It takes a special person to be able to do that, though." He eased forward and met her eyes. "Not everyone could remain calm in a time of distress. You're literally the lifeline to those people in need."

Lucy shrugged. She'd never thought of it that way, but he was correct. Still, she didn't take to praise very well. She was doing her job, helping others who couldn't help themselves, and she only hoped in some small way that she made a difference.

As more calls came through, she took them and talked to Noah in between. After about an hour, Officer McCoy came through to take Noah out on a call.

Part of Lucy hated to see him go, but the other part was relieved. She was having a difficult time sitting here ignoring his domineering presence.

As Noah stood up, he started to say something but a call came in and she tuned out everything else. This was going to be one of those nights where the phones were nonstop. Some days were like that and she was grateful she had something to occupy her time other than the mysterious new officer.

She wanted to know more about him, and living in this tiny town, she'd definitely find out. It wouldn't take long for the busybodies to be all abuzz with the backstory of their newest resident.

After they'd finished the call, which amounted to a couple of guys getting too rowdy outside of Gallagher's, the local bar, Noah climbed back into the patrol car. He wasn't used to riding on the passenger side, but he also wasn't used to this town, nor life without his ranch, not to mention life without his wife.

Each day was better than the last, but there was still that void he figured he'd always carry around.

Just as Officer McCoy started the car, Lucy's calm voice came over the radio.

"We've got a missing child at 186 Walnut Street.

The mother reported he was in his room and was supposed to be changing for bed, but now he's missing."

Just because he was a police officer didn't mean he didn't feel. Each case he encountered was different, and each one deserved his full attention and compassion. Noah's heart clenched at the fear that mother must be facing. He knew that fear of loss and the unknown.

"There's a creek that runs behind their house so the mother and some neighbors are there now," Lucy added.

McCoy turned on the siren and raced through the streets. Lucy's voice continued to keep them updated as she stayed on the line with a family friend. Lucy's sweet voice was exactly what he'd told her earlier—a lifeline. She was the link between the caller and the officers and she truly didn't see what an important job she had.

He should feel guilty thinking of her in any way except as a coworker, but there was something so innocent, yet so… He couldn't find the right word. Recognizable? Yes, definitely. He recognized the pain in her eyes, too. She did well to mask it, but it was there all the same. Perhaps she used that support group more for herself than she realized. And that was all fine and good, but talking among a group of strangers wasn't for him. He could get over his grief just fine on his own time.

Within minutes they were pulling up in front of

a small white cottage. Already people had congregated on the lawn. Adrenaline pumping, Noah raced toward the back of the house where he was told the mother was. McCoy went to talk to neighbors to get a description of the boy.

With the rains lately, the creek was up and Noah prayed this would only be a search and not a recovery.

Flashlights shifted all over the backyard, Noah's included. He tried to focus on the water, because if the boy was in there, he was in the most danger. Hopefully he was just in a neighbor's tree house or something that innocent and safe.

"He's there!" someone shouted. "He's caught under that shrub on the other side of the creek."

Noah followed the light stream from someone's flashlight. Immediately he took off running in the direction, his light bouncing as he ran faster.

He heard a woman scream and take off down the edge of the creek just in front of him. "Hold on, baby!"

Noah didn't think twice and he didn't stop to say anything. He raced past the frantic mother and the other people who were trying to figure out how to get the boy out.

As he ran into the cold water, Noah called out to the boy, "Hang on. I'm coming for you." The poor little guy was crying and the hood of his jacket had gotten caught on a dead limb sticking out from a bush along the creek side. His jacket was dark, but the bright yellow shirt made it a little easier for Noah to focus in on him.

The water was nearly to Noah's waist and colder than he'd initially thought. He didn't know how long the boy had been out here, but with the sun down, things had cooled off quite a bit.

The frantic mother continued to encourage her son to hang on as Noah trudged through the water. Blocking out all the chaos behind him, Noah focused solely on this boy.

"I've got you," Noah told him when he finally reached the child. "Wrap your legs around my waist and put your arms around my neck. I'm going to untangle your jacket."

The boy continued to cry and didn't move.

"My name is Officer Spencer, but you can call me Noah. What's your name?"

"C-Conner."

The boy's teeth were chattering. "Okay, Conner. I need you to be a big boy. I need a partner since my partner is in your house helping. Can you be my partner out here?"

Conner nodded. "I just wanted to see the storm and then I saw a c-cat run to the water. I wanted to s-save it."

"You're a brave boy, but right now I need you to wrap yourself around me so I can get you out of here. I don't know about you, but I think this water is cold."

Finally, little arms and legs went around Noah. Realizing the boy was about Emma's age, he felt a tug on his heart. Calls with kids always hit closer to home.

If he didn't get this jacket untangled in the next few seconds, Noah was going to cut it off. This boy had been waist deep in the water long enough. He shivered, not just from the cold, but from fear.

Finally, the material came free with a rip. Noah wasted no time. He waded back through the chilly water as the boy clung to him. On the bank, the crowd had grown and the mother stood sobbing, reaching her arms out, anxious to take her son.

The paramedics were right beside her, also ready to take the boy. Noah reached Conner out to his mom and climbed up the embankment. McCoy grabbed Noah's elbow to help him out.

The paramedics and the boy's mother were racing through the backyard, toward the driveway around front to the ambulance. The boy would be fine, but protocol required he get checked out. Noah would bet Conner wouldn't venture out to explore by himself anytime soon, and probably not near that creek for a long, long time.

"Good job, Spencer." McCoy slapped him on the back. "Already playing hero on your first serious call. You'll fit in just fine."

Noah smiled as they walked through the yard. He didn't want praise for doing his job, but he was glad he could help.

"At least the dip in the creek got the coffee off me," he joked.

McCoy laughed. "I thought you didn't get any coffee on you."

Noah shook his head. "I just told Lucy that so I wouldn't hurt her feelings. She'd already burned her hand and felt bad enough."

They reached the car and just as Noah pulled the handle, Conner's mother came up and wrapped her arms around him.

"Thank you," she cried, pulling back. "I promise I don't let him get near the creek. He's never done that before."

Noah placed a hand on her arm. "And I'm sure he won't do it again. You both had a scare, but you've got a brave boy. He wanted to see the storm and then tried to save a cat. You're doing a good job, mama. Kids are curious creatures by default."

She swiped the tears from her eyes and offered a smile before turning to go back to the waiting ambulance. Conner sat up on the cot inside the open doors and waved at Noah. Waving back, Noah offered his own grin.

Within minutes he and McCoy were headed back to the station where Noah could change and get dry. And see Lucy. On the short trip back, McCoy and Lucy exchanged some information about the boy being transported to the hospital.

Once again, her tone stirred something inside

Noah. Something he didn't want to address because he shouldn't be having these feelings. Should he?

He was human, he was a man, and he had natural desires. There was something about Lucy that made him not want to brush aside these unwanted emotions. No one had been able to reawaken the dead inside him for months. But whether it was her sweet voice, the compassion he already saw in her, or the underlying vulnerability she tried to hide, something about her drew him and made him want to get to know her more.

At this point, he figured they'd be seeing each other on a near daily basis. He might as well just roll with it and see what happened. But at the same time, he had to guard his heart. He was still healing, he was still in new territory…but he was also still fascinated by the gentle blonde with wide, expressive green eyes.

As they pulled into the station, Noah couldn't help but wonder what the next few days, weeks, and months would bring.

He hadn't known what to expect from this new town, but a reawakening in his desire certainly hadn't been on his list.

Chapter Three

Her nerves were near shot. Noah had been on the force for nearly a week and she'd worked five days out of the seven. Her usual part-time schedule had shifted into full-time since Carla had to be out with her mother for the next couple of weeks.

Which meant more face-to-face time with Officer Brooding and Sexy. Why, why, why did this man have to be the one she found so attractive? Why couldn't she get stirrings for a schoolteacher or a garbage man? A man who put his life on the line every day was an absolute no-no.

Her husband had done the same thing. Day after day he'd put himself out there...until one day he was gone.

Noah had only been on the force a short time and already he'd proven he was a man of loyalty, integrity, and compassion. He'd taken the little boy from the creek incident a stuffed animal before his shift. And the only reason anyone knew of that was because the mother called to tell Captain Cameron St. John what an amazing officer he had.

The back door opened and closed. Before she could turn to see which officer was coming on duty, a call came in. She pressed the key on the computer to answer and adjusted her headset.

"Stonerock Police Department."

"I have someone walking through my backyard carrying a baseball bat."

"Do you know who this person is?" Lucy replied.

"No, but they've been out there for a few minutes just staring at the house."

Lucy dispatched an officer and kept the caller on the line as she made sure the lady's doors were locked and she was away from doors and windows. The woman didn't sound frantic, but concerned.

Stonerock wasn't known for having many crimes, but there were crazy people everywhere. She couldn't take any call for granted.

Once the officer arrived and the caller confirmed it, Lucy disconnected the call. When she turned in her seat, she was alone in the room, but she knew who'd come in earlier. That aftershave still permeating the room had become so familiar, making her insides stir and get all schoolgirl giddy.

She was a grown woman getting giddy. How sad was that?

Keeping her feelings in check was the smart thing to do. She needed to keep her emotional distance from Noah, but each day she saw him, she realized she wanted to see more of him, to learn more about him. That need was a recipe for disaster and heartache. Neither of them was at a place in their lives to act on attraction. Of course, she was still assuming it was one-sided, which was all the more reason for her to rein in her school-girl crush.

Only this didn't feel like anything she'd had as a teenager. Her attraction for Noah Spencer was all grown up…as were the dreams she'd been having since that first meeting in the rain.

Lucy came to her feet and stretched her neck from side to side. She was pulling a double shift today, which was fine. She could use the extra money to put back into the support group fund. Tonight was a meeting, but Kate and Tara were fine without her. It's not like Lucy was ever missed.

"Thought you were off today."

She jerked around to see Noah standing in the doorway drinking a cup of coffee. His dark eyes held hers and she had to force herself to not fidget.

"Taking on a few more shifts while Carla is out. I can always use extra money for my group."

His dark brows drew in. "Aren't you missing a meeting tonight?"

Lucy shrugged. "I am, but my girls understand. Sometimes we have to cover for each other."

He took a sip of coffee from one of the disposable cups. When he pushed off the doorway, Lucy thought he was about to turn and leave, but he crossed the room and headed for her desk. Lucy spun around, pretending to stare at the monitors. It was a slow night, but she still wished for a call to come in right then. She couldn't handle all this tension. Well, the tension on her part at least. She never could get a grasp on what he was feeling.

"What do you do in your spare time?" he asked as he took a seat beside her.

The question threw her off as she glanced to the clock. He was early for his shift by about twenty minutes. Why was he choosing to sit in here with her?

"Spare time?" she asked, fidgeting with her watch. "I'm usually looking for speakers for the group or community projects we can do. Giving back and lifting others up is a great way to—"

"No."

Lucy jerked her attention back to him. "What do you mean, no?"

Noah set his cup on the desk and leaned forward. That dark stare of his zeroed in on her and she could easily see him cornering a suspect with those eyes, or seducing a woman. Those eyes held every secret, letting no emotion slip through. That whole guarded, sultry thing he had going might be the sexiest thing she'd ever seen in her life.

The uniform didn't hurt, either. But she'd rather have a man not so committed to danger and more committed to…well, her. As selfish as that sounded, part of her hated knowing that her husband had sacrificed his life defending their country, but that was the type of man he'd been. And she could tell that was the type of man Noah was.

"I know you work and volunteer your time for the group," he stated, still holding her in place with that mesmerizing gaze. "But I'm asking what else you do."

"Oh, I study. I'm almost done with my online classes."

Noah shook his head. "For fun. What do you do for fun?"

Lucy opened her mouth, then shut it. She thought for a second, but nothing came to her. Surely she'd done something for fun lately…hadn't she? Her friends were always texting her or calling for some reason or another. But she couldn't recall the last time they went out and did anything.

"I have horses," she replied. "Two of them. They were my husband's, so they're mine now."

Before she could even think of something she actually did just for herself, a call came in. It took great effort on her part, but she blocked out the presence of the powerful man beside her. The call didn't take long and didn't require anyone to be dispatched. An elderly lady had locked herself out of her home, but ended up finding her key in the bottom of her purse while she was talking.

When Lucy disconnected the call, Officer McCoy came in the back door. "Evening. Gettin' chilly out there."

Noah spun in the chair. "It's downright frigid to me. I guess I'll have to invest in thicker coats."

"Drink more coffee," McCoy suggested as he passed on through to the break room.

"It's not too bad here," Lucy replied once Noah turned back to her. "But I guess coming from Texas, Stonerock does seem cold in the fall."

"Everything is different from Texas," he muttered.

There went that darkness settling over him again. If she could just break through…but that would require her getting closer and spending more time with him. That probably wasn't smart. Maybe she should have Tara or Kate reach out to Noah. Definitely a better option.

A sliver of jealousy speared through her at the idea of her friends getting one-on-one time with Noah.

"Are you upset about missing the meeting?" he asked.

Lucy tipped her head and eased back in her chair. "Why would you say that?"

"Because you've looked upset since I walked in."

Upset? That's what he got out of her appearance and attitude? She was seriously out of practice. Granted, she'd never had to initiate conversation or flirting with a man. Evan had asked her out and he'd taken charge. He was her first love, so...yeah, right now she was seriously out of her element. Maybe she should give up and stop trying. Had she even started, though?

"I'm not upset," she assured him.

Noah grabbed his cup, but never took his eyes off her. "You hide it well, but something is bothering you. None of my business, though."

He rose to his feet and turned to leave the room.

"Wait a minute," she called. "You're the one who seems all brooding and quiet. Over the past week you've barely said a word to me other than hi and bye. You talk to everyone else but me."

Noah glanced over his shoulder. "I speak with you over the radio every day."

Yeah, and that grated on her nerves because his low, gravelly voice always made her tingle and she did not want to tingle. Damn it, she didn't know what she wanted, but she at least wanted him to stop torturing her. Maybe acknowledge her as more than an annoyance or someone not to be bothered with. But the casual greeting as he came and went didn't sit well with her.

Well, maybe she wouldn't mind so much if he

did the same to everyone, but it was only her as far as she could tell. Had she done something to offend him? How was that even possible when she'd barely spoken to him other than to dispatch calls through the radio?

"Face-to-face, you ignore me." That sounded so childish. Lucy came to her feet and sighed. "We're like a family here, so I don't want any tension."

Noah shifted to face her fully. "Are you feeling tension?"

She was feeling sexually frustrated, but she figured announcing that wasn't professional. Was this what it would be like getting back into the dating world? She wasn't so sure she was up for this game.

Instead of answering his question, she asked one of her own. "Are you telling me you aren't?"

Shut up, Lucy. Just shut up.

"Because I don't try to cover my feelings," she went on, ignoring that inner voice. "Attraction is a natural emotion."

When his eyes widened, she seriously wanted to die. He seemed shocked, whether at her blunt statement or the fact he wasn't feeling the same, she had no clue. Regardless, it was out there now and she really, really wished she didn't always take the advice of her therapist and tell people how she felt.

McCoy came back through, whistling and holding his own cup of coffee. At the same time, another call rang through the room, effectively severing the awkward silence that had descended since she'd opened her mouth and opted to pour out her thoughts.

Lucy took the interruption as a sign that it was indeed time to shut up and stop telling Noah…well, anything. She quickly answered the call and sat back down at her desk. By the time she was done, Noah and Sergeant McCoy were gone and Lucy's heart was still beating like mad.

She'd stepped over some professional boundary and she had no clue how to come back from that. Noah was now well aware of how she felt about him, and from the look on his face, he didn't want to accept it.

Fantastic. How on earth did she come back from this embarrassing moment?

Okay, cooking wasn't necessarily her thing. Actually, she was terrible at it. But Lucy knew how to bake and actually loved doing it.

Which was why she found herself standing on the porch of one adorable little gray-and-white cottage on the edge of town. Lucy secured the basket of cranberry scones under one arm and rang the doorbell with her free hand.

Nerves gathered in her belly and she couldn't believe she was actually standing here. Hadn't she made a big enough fool of herself yesterday? At work, no less.

Maybe she should just leave the basket on the swing and—

The door opened, cutting off her thoughts. Once she recovered from the fact she was actually at Noah's home, it took every single ounce of self-restraint she had not to burst out laughing.

"Are you wearing—"

"Yes. What are you doing here?"

Lucy didn't know whether to be extremely confused or thoroughly entertained at the sight of Noah Spencer sporting a plastic tiara, dangling clip-on jeweled earrings, and a purple beaded necklace.

Before Lucy could make a comment of any sort, a little girl popped out from behind Noah's legs. She too wore fancy accessories, but she had on a sparkly dress with a full skirt that went all the way to the floor.

Lucy immediately glanced back to Noah. He offered a simple smile, flashing that dimple at the corner of his mouth.

"This is my daughter, Emma. Emma, this is one of Daddy's coworkers, Lucy."

His daughter. Lucy hadn't heard a word about a little girl. Noah was one private man and now Lucy felt even sillier coming here unannounced.

"You look beautiful," Lucy stated as she bent down to the pre-schooler. "Do you always play dress-up with your dad?"

"I played with my mommy, but she's not here anymore." Emma's little chin wobbled for a second before she continued. "Daddy lets me put anything on him, but not a dress."

Lucy laughed. Apparently Noah had his limits even with his little girl.

Emma smiled up at her dad and Noah nodded to her. When the little girl turned her wide blue eyes back to Lucy, Lucy couldn't help but smile in return.

"We have tea parties," Emma answered. "Daddy puts extra sugar in it."

As she spoke again, Lucy realized the little girl had the cutest dimple on the side of her mouth, just like her father. Could she be any more adorable?

A flash of old dreams coursed through Lucy's mind. At one time she and Evan had wanted children. They'd bought their home with all the acreage and added two horses, with the intention of filling their home with kids. Then he'd been deployed and that had been the end of her dreams for a family.

She'd always assumed those wishes had died with him, but seeing little Emma brought them back again. A lump settled in her throat, blocking her words.

"Come on in." Noah stepped back, placing a hand on Emma's shoulder to pull her with him. "Sorry. It's cold out there."

Lucy stepped over the threshold and attempted a smile to mask the unexpected hurt. "You've just got to get that Southern blood used to this. It's really not cold in the grand scheme of things."

He grunted as he shut the door. Emma ran through the house and disappeared, apparently getting back to her interrupted tea party. Lucy clutched her basket as more doubts crept in.

"I'm sorry," she began as she turned back to Noah. "I shouldn't just show up unannounced. Especially after yesterday, but… You know, it's really difficult to talk to you when you're dressed like an overgrown princess."

Noah pulled the tiara from his head and snapped the earrings off his ears, but remained in the beads. "What brought you here, Lucy?"

Was it completely pathetic that she liked how he said her name? Most likely, but she couldn't help how she felt. She could, however, keep her mouth shut on that subject and try to get back on some level ground with him.

"I made scones for you." She held up the basket and smiled. "I didn't know you had a little girl or I would've made some of my monster cookies."

"Monster cookies?" he asked as he used his fingertip to push aside the checkered towel to see inside the basket.

"It's a chocolate chip cookie, but you add M&M's and other candies. Really, anything you like. They're pretty amazing."

He pulled a scone from the basket and took a bite. When his lids lowered and he groaned, Lucy felt more confident in her decision to bring the peace offering. She typically only baked for the support group or for family and friends. This was the first time she'd done it for a virtual stranger.

"These are amazing," he said around his second bite. "Is that cranberry?"

"It is, and I put a dash of orange in it."

He finished the scone and dusted his hand on his jeans. "You might as well come on in, but I can't guarantee you won't end up with a tiara on your head and a cup of tea."

A little part of Lucy's heart flipped over.

"I'd love to have a tiara."

Noah reached for the basket. "Come on back."

"Wait." She relinquished the basket and shoved her hands inside her jacket. "I want to apologize for yesterday. I didn't mean to make things uncomfortable between us."

The dark eyes she'd come to appreciate held her as he closed the distance between them. In one hand he held the basket, and in the other he had the girly accessories.

"I wasn't uncomfortable," he murmured. "Intrigued and surprised, but not uncomfortable."

The air between them seemed to thicken because she was having a difficult time breathing. And he still appeared just as calm and in control as ever.

"Why don't you take your jacket off and join our tea party?" he asked.

Lucy couldn't help the nervous laugh that escaped

her lips. "How can I turn down an invitation like that from a man wearing purple beads?"

Emma came twirling back through the house holding a stuffed bear as her dance partner. "Is the pretty lady staying?"

Lucy kept her focus on Noah because that precious girl was a reminder of things she'd once dreamed of. Things Lucy hadn't realized she still wanted until just now. A child of her own. A family.

Honestly, Lucy didn't know what was more damaging to her heart, Emma or Noah. But the combination of the two was downright terrifying. Nevertheless, she wasn't going to pass up the chance to stay.

Part of her rationalized that she was staying as a way to break through to Noah and get him to open up about his feelings. He needed new friends in the town, right? And since he refused to join her meetings, she'd just have to try to get him to open up in other ways. She could be his support team…right? That was totally logical and the right thing to do.

Of course the devil on her other shoulder called her a bald-faced liar. She was staying because she was on this roller coaster of newfound emotions and she had no clue how to stop the ride…or even if she wanted to stop it.

As crazy as it sounded, Noah had reawakened something deep inside her. For two years she'd focused on throwing herself into work, the group, school.

But now maybe she just wanted to be selfish and see what happened.

"I'm staying," Lucy replied as she smiled back to Emma.

The little girl bounced up and down, sending her blond curls dancing around her shoulders. "Yay. I'll have Mr. Bear sit on my lap and you can have his chair."

She scurried off just as fast as she'd entered and Noah shook his head. "You should feel honored. I've never had Mr. Bear's seat."

Lucy slid out of her jacket and hung it on the hook by the door. She completely ignored the fact it was nestled between a tiny pink-and-white polka-dot coat and a large black woolen one. Well, she tried to anyway.

She was seeing a whole new side to Noah she hadn't even known existed, but she liked it. The idea that he was a single father really helped Lucy understand why he'd been so reserved. The man had lost his wife and was protecting all the life he had left.

She could spend all day analyzing this situation from his angle, from hers, but right now she was going to enjoy the moment. She'd have time to analyze it later.

What the hell was he thinking? He should never have let Lucy inside his home. Granted he'd only been here a couple weeks, but this was his home now.

Having Lucy here botched up his plans to keep his life simple and his heart guarded.

But damn, that scone was something else. He hadn't had something that delicious and homemade in…well, ever. His wife hadn't been much of a cook, but that never bothered him. They mostly lived off the ranch anyway, between the livestock and the fields. Noah had cooked, too, taking pity on Cara who panicked at the sight of a recipe or the thought of a casserole.

This new lifestyle was taking some serious getting used to. Between the cooler weather, the free time he had from not ranching, and acclimating to the new force, his entire world had been reshaped. But he was grateful he had a job, a home, and his daughter. They'd make it because he was determined to give her the best life possible, considering the circumstances.

"Want to see my room?" Emma asked Lucy.

Without waiting for a reply, Emma hopped up from her little chair and grabbed Lucy's hand.

"Calm down, Em." Noah finished clearing the tea set from the table. "Maybe Lucy has somewhere else to be. She hadn't exactly planned on staying here today."

Lucy held Emma's hand and stood. "I'd love to see your room."

"My daddy painted it just like I wanted," Emma

chattered as she led Lucy away. "And then he put up this sparkly light and…"

Her voice trailed away and Noah glanced to the clock. It was almost time for him to lie down and get a few hours' sleep before going into work later tonight. The realtor had suggested a fabulous babysitter that lived only two doors down: a retired lady who was known as the town grandma and had babysat for years. Having someone dependable and trustworthy made this entire process much less stressful. Each little layer of his new life that fell into place where he needed eased his worry.

Noah wondered if he'd see Lucy at work, but then quickly pushed the thought aside. She'd been here for over an hour and if he was already looking forward to seeing her again, then he was falling down that rabbit hole he never wanted to be near again.

He wasn't ready to move on. Cara had been gone only six months. Shouldn't he wait longer before allowing that desire to creep in? Not that he'd let this happen. He looked at Lucy and…well, his thoughts, emotions and feelings had slipped from his control.

Noah rinsed out the tea set and put it away. Tea parties were a thing his wife had started with Emma and he'd wanted to keep some sense of normalcy in her life. As soon as they hit town, he took her shopping for a new tea set and they'd had a party every single day since. He didn't mind dressing up so long as it put a smile on Emma's face.

When they were gone a lengthy amount of time, Noah figured he'd better go save Lucy because Emma hadn't been around a woman, minus the sitter, since her mother passed. She was most likely craving that connection. Both of Cara's parents were gone and so was Noah's mother…he'd never known his father.

Noah reached the doorway and found Emma and Lucy on the widow seat. Emma had already draped necklaces and headbands on Lucy.

"Oh, honey. Maybe Lucy didn't want to be covered in accessories."

Lucy picked up another hair ribbon. "Actually, it's been a long time since someone pampered me. I was rather enjoying myself."

The sight of Emma with another young woman, and not his late wife, did something to him. Something he couldn't quite pinpoint. On one hand, there was that ever-pressing remorse he carried. The guilt of getting on with his life. The guilt of not having been able to save his wife.

He'd been a police officer back in Texas as well and had saved others, but ultimately he hadn't been able to save his own wife. He'd spoken to her after the storm and she'd assured him she was fine, but he should have—

He stopped himself. The blame would never end.

On the other hand, he knew his wife would've wanted him to move on, to live for their daughter.

She wouldn't like that he was feeling guilt, because that emotion robbed his happiness.

"I hate to break up this party, but it's time for you to go to Miss Mary's house."

Emma protested with a whine, but Lucy placed a hand on her knee. "It's okay. Maybe we can have another playdate."

"Really?" Emma asked, suddenly in a better mood.

Lucy glanced to Noah. "If your dad doesn't mind."

Noah weighed the options. He didn't want to let this get too routine because Emma would likely get attached. He had to watch out for her, but on the other hand, it was nice to see his daughter open up and want to play and be with another young woman.

He couldn't lie—seeing them together put his guard up. He wasn't looking for a replacement for his wife or mother for his child. At this point, he wasn't looking for anything because he was still trying to figure out this new life.

A mix of emotions swirled through him. He was attracted to Lucy and he had to assume that was normal, but that didn't mean he felt good about it. It didn't mean it was right to happen at this particular moment.

"I'm pretty busy, though." Lucy glanced to Noah and back to Emma. "I'll talk to your dad later at work and we'll see. Okay?"

Lucy took off all of her play jewelry and hair accessories. After laying them on the window seat, she bent down to Emma.

"Thank you so much for showing me your room. It is beautiful just like you. Maybe one day you could come see my horses since I know you miss yours."

Emma squealed. "Can I, Daddy? Please, please, please."

Noah laughed. "We'll see what we can work out."

Emma threw her arms around Lucy's neck and Noah had to look away. He couldn't see this, couldn't let his heart flip over in his chest. He loved Emma with everything he had in him, but Lucy was practically a stranger.

Maybe he needed distance himself, because the more he was around Lucy with her sweet smile and her easygoing nature, the more he wanted to be. And the fact she'd brought him a peace offering wasn't helping the case he was trying to make regarding staying emotionally detached.

Lucy had enjoyed a tea party, she'd played dress-up, and she'd baked him scones. And that was only in a little over an hour. What would happen if he invited her back for dinner? Or if they went to a movie or to the park? Then what? Would he grow even more intrigued?

Lucy crossed the room toward him and Noah had to shift out of the doorway so she could pass. When she got within a few inches, she paused and looked him straight in the eye.

"Thanks for sharing your day with me," she said. "That meant more than you know."

And then she was walking down the hall and out the door. That was the end of it.

Or was it? Because the sadness in her eyes when she'd thanked him had him wanting to run after her and figure out just what was hurting her. But he didn't, because he knew her angle. Yes, the attraction was there, but she wanted to cure him or make his life better. She'd mentioned her group more than once and she was the type of person who would throw herself into helping others and forgetting herself.

The unmistakable sorrow he'd glimpsed as she passed by couldn't be ignored, but it wouldn't be easy to bring up at work when he went in for his shift. There were other officers coming and going and calls she'd be taking. But he'd find a way.

Lucy may think she was going to cure him, but perhaps it wasn't he who needed the help.

Chapter Four

"You don't actually believe we're going to let you off the hook, right?"

Lucy was hoping for exactly that. She set the mugs of hot chocolate topped with whipped cream down on the coffee table and Tara and Kate each reached for theirs. This was Lucy's first night off in days and she wanted nothing more than to wear her fat sweatpants and no bra, and have some sugary drink with her friends.

The hot chocolate wasn't even spiked. Kate's parents had been killed by a drunk driver, so she didn't drink, and Tara and Lucy respected her enough to not drink in her presence.

"We'll hang around long enough and she'll be chatty. She won't be able to keep it inside."

Lucy rolled her eyes at Tara. "I'm not going to get chatty. There's nothing to tell, really."

"I heard you were at Officer Spencer's house yesterday afternoon," Kate stated as she held her moose mug with both hands.

They'd gathered at Lucy's house, in agreement they were going to stay in, binge watch romantic comedies, and have some downtime. They were all so busy with their own work lives lately that it wasn't often they could meet outside of the support group.

But here they were and Lucy was being quizzed, all because Noah lived on a street with busybody neighbors. And it wasn't like anything had happened. She'd drunk tea; she'd played for a while with Emma. End of story.

Right?

"What's that look on her face?" Kate whispered to Tara.

"I think she's trying to find a way not to answer our questions."

Lucy laughed. "Would you two knock it off? I was at Noah's house, but just to take him some scones."

"The cranberry orange ones?" Tara asked. "Those are the best things you make. You must really be interested in him."

Lucy didn't take the bait. She should've known girls' night in would turn into her best friends teaming up against her. Though, if the tables were reversed, she'd be doing the same. Still, she didn't want to talk about Noah. There wasn't really much to say. She'd seen a spark of interest, but at the same time, he'd also kept that guard up.

Even at work that evening, he'd entered with another officer coming on duty. They'd all made small talk and then the guys had been dispatched. After that, their only conversations had been emergency calls on the radio.

And now she was off for the next two nights. She wasn't sure if he was or not, but she didn't ask. She'd gotten done what she set out to do and that was apologize for making things seem unprofessional.

"So what's his story?" Kate asked. "Because the town is starting to make up their own about him. I heard he has a cute little girl."

Lucy nodded. "Emma. She's four."

Tara curled her legs to her side on the couch as she reached for her drink. "And he's a widower?"

"Yeah. His wife passed away during a storm when they lived in Texas. I heard he was a rancher and an officer, but he hasn't said any of that to me. He's pretty private."

"Yet you were in his home, with his child, for what? An hour?"

Lucy met Kate's raised brow and knowing grin. "Exactly. His child was home. We work together, for pity's sake. Nothing is happening."

"Not yet," Kate muttered around her mug.

Okay, it was time to steer the conversation away from herself because as much as she'd like for something to happen with the new officer, she wasn't holding her breath.

"Are we still on for dancing tomorrow night at Gallagher's?" Lucy asked as she licked the point off her whip cream.

Tara nodded. "Marley is with her dad, so I'm game."

Tara and her husband, Sam, hadn't been married long when they realized they didn't want the same things out of life. They'd married after a whirlwind affair and amazing chemistry, but marriages were based on so much more.

Being a single mom was difficult for Tara, but she and her ex managed to get along and put the needs of their daughter, Marley, first.

Lucy and her best friends all faced different obstacles and trials in their lives. They'd been friends since grade school when Lucy had cut off Kate's pigtails with her new sharp scissors. Kate had wanted her hair cut and her mother had kept saying no, so Kate had actually been grateful to Lucy. That same year, Tara had moved to town and the three just clicked. They'd been through it all together and always had each other's backs.

"I love going to Gray's place." Tara swiped her finger through her whip cream and licked it off. "We may be the only ones who go there just to dance. But

Gray Gallagher has taken that bar and made it even more popular than ever."

The local bar was in its third generation and currently owned by one of their good friends. Gray Gallagher was such a great guy and no doubt one of the reasons why so many women flocked to the place on ladies' night. Gray had always been that fun guy with a sexy build. When he'd come home from the Army, he'd immediately taken over Gallagher's from his father, but he'd yet to settle down.

Because isn't that what people did in this small town? They came home after college or the military and immediately met the love of their life, married, settled down and had babies. Or so the myth went. But not every life was so picture-perfect and neat and tidy.

Sometimes tragedies happened, lives were ripped apart. And sometimes something positive could stem from such tragedies. Lucy, Kate and Tara were dedicating their lives to making a change in this community. They all had their own type of heartache and voids in their lives which made them perfect to work together and comfort others.

Too often when someone suffered loss, people around them didn't know how to respond or what to say, so they just tiptoed around the delicate topic.

Lucy knew firsthand that didn't help the person suffering; it only made things more uncomfortable. Which was why she and her friends were going to start opening their doors to everyone at the meetings of their support group. Even if someone hadn't dealt with the death of a loved one, they still knew people who had, and Lucy wanted them to know how to handle those who grieved.

"I guess we should discuss the upcoming meeting since we're going to be out dancing tomorrow," Lucy stated.

"Are we done discussing your police officer?" Kate asked. "Because I don't really feel like we got much information."

"You got all the info you need." Lucy set her mug back on the tray. "We should go ahead and plan on about fifty people. That's aiming high, but I'd rather be over-prepared than under."

The more they discussed, the more their plans fell into place, and Lucy breathed a sigh of relief that they'd moved on from the topic of her personal life. She wasn't dumb enough to believe they'd dropped it for good, but at least for now she was safe.

All Lucy had to do was remember that Noah wasn't looking for anyone. And hadn't she told herself she wasn't looking, either? Yet here she was constantly thinking about him.

So what did she do? Ignore her feelings or act on them? The risk of acting and being seen as a fool put a newfound fear in her. She'd never approached a man before, but since she'd already broached that territory with him, she figured she'd have to keep riding this out.

But the ball was in his court, so to speak. The question was, would he do anything with it?

The annual fall festival was in just a few days and Noah knew he'd be working security there. Not that Stonerock was known for major crime, but security at any event was imperative.

He'd heard chatter about how amazing this festival was and how the entire town came out for it. Captain St. John had already told Noah they'd be working the same shift. Thankfully the sitter was going to bring Emma over for a little while. There would be face painting, bake sales, games, a few small rides, music, and in the evenings a big bonfire. He'd heard there was an area set up with a guy who cooked beans all day in a pot over the fire and served them up during the bonfire.

Noah was really starting to feel at home here. Nothing was the same as his ranch in Texas, but the familiarity of working on a force helped ease him into this new chapter in his life. The small town was exactly what he and Emma needed to feel like they were part of something and it wasn't just them trying to survive. She'd already made friends with some children from the sitter and he…well, he guessed he made some friends, too.

Was that what he was calling Lucy? His friend? Because he'd had female friends back in Texas and not one of them made him anxious and excited at just the mere thought of them.

Noah yawned as he grabbed his keys and started for the back door of the station. His shift was over and they'd been so slow during the night, the hours seemed to drag. And idle time was never good for someone grieving...or someone having guilt for fantasizing about another woman.

A huge part of him felt like he was cheating on his wife, but the other part of him knew he had to move on. He couldn't control his feelings and he sure as hell hadn't picked whom he was attracted to.

As he headed to his truck, he spotted Lucy in the front seat of her car. Her head was on the steering wheel. Alarm hit him first. Was she sick? Passed out?

He crossed the lot to the side of her car and gently tapped on the window. When she jerked in her seat and turned toward him, he instantly saw she was upset. Tears streamed down her face as she rolled her window down.

"What happened?" he asked, resting his hands on the door so he could lean down.

She swiped at her damp cheeks. "It's nothing. I just needed a minute."

Noah leaned down farther, resting his arm on the door. "It's obviously something, since it made you cry."

Her bright eyes seemed to sparkle even more with

unshed tears. "One of the ladies who comes to the meetings lost her dog."

A rancher at heart, Noah was an animal lover, but for Lucy to get this upset over someone else's animal was rather surprising.

"Sorry," she said with a sniff as she waved her hand as if to blow off her emotions. "It's just that Tammy bought this dog after her husband passed away last year because she wanted the company. But he got out of the house and was hit by a school bus. I just hung up with her and she's so upset."

As much as he felt terrible for this stranger, there was a stirring deep within him for the amount of sympathy Lucy had for the people in her group. Lucy cared with her whole heart. He heard it each time she came over the radio to him, he saw it in the way she was with his daughter, and now how she grieved for a widowed lady's dog.

"You going to be okay to drive home?" he asked.

Lucy nodded. "I'll be fine. I'm going to swing by her place to check on her. I don't want her to be alone right now."

Of course she wasn't going home. She'd only worked all night and had been pulling double shifts, not to mention whatever hours she logged into her schoolwork.

"It's not safe for you to be on the roads when you're this tired."

Defying him, she started her car. "I'm fine, Noah.

I'll take ten minutes to check on Tammy and then I'll go home."

Noah didn't bother backing away or even attempting to move. She glared in his direction and raised one brow as if to dare him to say another word. Whatever she did on her time off wasn't his concern, but at the same time, they were friends. Right?

"As your friend, I'm going to give you some advice."

Lucy gripped the steering wheel and stared at her hands. "A friend?" she asked, glancing back to him. "Fine. If that's how you want to play this out."

She was going to be difficult. She couldn't just let this ride out, but he wasn't taking her bait.

"Go home and rest," he advised. "When you wake up, take her some of those amazing scones or something else you bake and then you'll have time to visit and not feel rushed."

Lucy pursed her lips and he was shocked she seemed to be thinking about his suggestion instead of instantly arguing.

"Fine."

Noah stood straight up. "What?"

"Oh, don't look so surprised that I agreed," she scolded. "Your idea makes more sense. I just… I want to fix it now for her. I hate knowing people I care about are hurting. It hurts me. My heart literally aches for her."

Noah swallowed, hating the lump that formed in

his own throat. An image of Lucy going through her own grief didn't sit well with him. Who did she have? Oh, she had her friends, but what family? Because he'd never heard her discuss any. Not that they'd talked a lot, but still. In general conversation most people brought up parents or siblings. She'd only talked about her friends who helped her with the support group.

He didn't like that she gave everything to everyone and went home to a lonely house. But, again, that wasn't his business. Damn it, though, he wanted to do something. What would he do? Ask her to come over again? That wasn't smart. Having Lucy in his house was just adding another layer to this already complicated situation. His life didn't need anything else that was new and out of his comfort zone.

But Lucy didn't exactly make him uncomfortable. She made him achy, needy, wanting.

"Why don't you come over?" he asked before he could stop himself. Shoving his hands in his jacket pocket, he shrugged. "Emma would like to see you again."

Lame, Spencer. Totally lame.

"Would she?" Lucy asked, her mouth tipping up into a soft smile. "Well, I'd like to see her again."

Nodding, Noah stepped back, realizing he'd already opted to dive headfirst into this. When she continued to smile at him, he felt a stirring somewhere deep in his chest. Someplace that had been dead so long, he'd almost forgotten it existed.

"Then I'll see you later," he told her as he crossed the lot to his truck. By the time he got in and started his engine, Lucy sat in her car smiling over at him.

Whatever he'd gotten himself into was nobody's fault but his at this point. So, here he was about to have a woman to his house. A woman he'd invited under the pretense of seeing his daughter. But he was a fool and Lucy had seen right through him.

If he was going to continue on this unknown journey, he was going to have to become a stronger man, at least where Lucy was concerned, because she was quickly wearing him down.

Chapter Five

"Thanks, Captain."

Captain Cameron St. John nodded. "No need to thank me, Lucy. I'm sorry about your car."

She didn't even want to look around the captain at the sight of her car being pulled away by the wrecker. She'd just left the station and had been heading home, as she'd promised, but someone had run a red light and T-boned her car. Her car she had just paid off.

Her hands still shook and she wasn't sure she was ready to get out of the captain's patrol car yet, either. She'd never been in an accident, and she was quite certain she never wanted to be in another.

"It's a little different being on this side of the job," she stated, trying to get her heartbeat back to normal.

"I just wish we knew who hit you," Cameron muttered. "I've got some patrolmen driving around looking. Whoever it was has some massive damage to their car, so they should be easy to spot."

Lucy blew out a sigh. "I'm sorry. It all happened so fast and all I saw was a dark color fleeing the scene."

Cameron patted her shoulder. "It's all right. We take care of our own."

She loved that about her job. They were like family. Still, she wished her car weren't smashed because she had no backup. Lucy rubbed her forehead, trying to ward off a headache.

"You sure you don't want the EMTs to check you out?" he asked.

Lucy shook her head. "No. I'll be fine. I could use a lift home, though."

"No problem."

Cameron drove her home, which wasn't far considering she was only a few miles away when she was hit. During the ride she asked about his family and if they were all bringing their kids to the fall festival. Cameron had two brothers and they were all influential people in the town.

"If you need to call out tomorrow, don't think anything about it."

He pulled into her drive and Lucy grabbed her purse. "Thanks, but I'm sure I'll be all right. Besides, Carla is still out."

"I think she'll be back tomorrow," he told her.

Tugging on her handle, she smiled. "Well, I can still come to work. I wasn't injured, just shaken up and a little sore on my left side where I hit the door."

Cameron nodded. "The offer still stands."

"Thanks for the ride," she told him as she got out.

As she let herself in her back door, her cell chimed, but she was juggling her key in the lock and holding her purse. She let it go to voice mail; it wasn't like she was in the mood to talk anyway.

As soon as she stepped inside and dropped her purse to the counter, the phone started ringing again. All she wanted to do was grab a quick shower and crawl into bed. Or maybe she'd just go straight to bed.

Lucy's mind raced as she thought of getting some much-needed sleep, then getting up to bake something to take to Tammy, who'd just lost her pup.

First thing after she woke she needed to see to the horses and make sure they had enough straw and water. They should be fine, but she tended to them every single day just like Evan used to do.

Oh, yeah. Then after all of that she had an invitation to Noah's house. She may cancel that because... well, she was exhausted and sore and perhaps she shouldn't keep going around sweet, impressionable Emma. The little girl had recently lost her mother and Lucy wasn't sure of the circumstances surrounding that tragedy. But Noah had invited her over, so perhaps he wanted to grab that olive branch she'd extended. Maybe he needed a friend. But part of Lucy didn't want to just be a friend to the only man she'd felt a pull toward since her husband passed.

Though there was more time since her tragic loss than his, she knew grief couldn't be given a time frame. Everyone healed differently and everyone moved on at their own pace.

Lucy locked her back door and wondered what she'd do about wheels. On a groan, she realized she wouldn't be going anywhere with baked goods. Perhaps she could call Tammy and invite her over. Maybe getting her out of the house would be a good idea, because that's the only way Lucy was going to be able to try to comfort her in person.

And she surely wasn't about to ask Noah to give her a lift. Speaking of Noah, she'd best send him a text and tell him she couldn't make it later that day.

As she headed through her one-story house, she started stripping out of her clothes. By the time she reached her bedroom, she was ready to put on her favorite ratty nightgown, draw her room-darkening shades, and crawl into bed. She'd worked midnights for so long, she had her system down pat. Her bedroom was in the back of the house, away from any road traffic, and when her door was shut and her fan was on, it was out of earshot of the doorbell.

Lucy tossed her clothes into the basket and had just pulled her nightgown over her head when the doorbell rang. Seriously? She should've turned her fan on and shut the door right away.

She started to climb into bed, more than willing to ignore the unwanted guest. Her neighbors knew she worked midnights, so they never bothered her. But the doorbell turned to a persistent knock.

Obviously someone needed her right now. Since her nightgown was an oversize T-shirt style that hit her knees, she didn't bother with clothes. She'd get rid of this person and get into bed.

Lucy padded down the hallway and came to the small foyer. Even through the etched glass of her front door she recognized that shape. What was he doing here?

Flicking the lock on the door, she opened it and didn't get a chance to say a word as Noah stepped right up to her. His eyes raked over her, his hands falling to her shoulders.

"Why aren't you at the hospital getting checked out?"

She should've known the accident wouldn't remain quiet. Not in a small town with a small police force who knew each other's business.

"Because you told me to come straight home to bed," she countered. "Which I was trying to do."

His brows drew in. "Don't be sarcastic. Cameron said you wouldn't go get checked out."

The captain was the snitch? No, she didn't believe that for a minute. Regardless, this wasn't Noah's business. He couldn't ignore her and then suddenly show up at her door like he had a right to be concerned.

"Shouldn't you be home?" she asked, wondering when he was going to remove his hands from her shoulders. Not that she wanted him to.

The fact he rushed here and was worried spoke volumes about the feelings he went out of his way to fight off.

"I'd just gotten home and changed when I heard the call over the scanner," he replied as he eased her into her house and closed the door behind him. "A hit-and-run?"

Lucy nodded. "Yeah. Some jerk totaled my car."

"Did you get a look at the vehicle or the driver?"

Shrugging her sore shoulders, Lucy shook her head. "No. Just that the car was dark colored. It happened so fast. Thankfully I'm not hurt, just sore. My hip is a little bruised. This guy is going to have a rough time hiding with a banged-up car."

Noah raked his hand through his dark hair. "There's only going to be one dark-colored vehicle that is mangled in the front in a town this small."

Lucy noticed he kept fidgeting. Glancing her way, running his hand over his stubbled jawline and his fingers through his hair.

"You all right?" she asked.

Noah laughed as he turned his focus solely to her. "You're kidding, right? I heard you had been in an accident, a hit-and-run, and I worried. So I called the station and they said Cameron was on the scene and the EMTs had been sent away. So, no, I'm not all right because you could be hurt and not know it. Internal injuries can be well hidden."

When Lucy went to reach for him, she felt a pain in her back and she hissed.

"Damn it." Noah wrapped his arms around her and gently picked her up. "You need to be seen."

"No, I need to be in bed." Just as soon as she finished being carried like some helpless heroine in a historical novel. "I need to take some pain reliever, get some rest, and maybe soak in a hot bath later. That's all."

"Why are you so stubborn?" he muttered as he headed down the hallway. "Which one is your room?"

"As flattered as I am at your seduction, I'm afraid I'm not up to a romp right now."

Noah's glare told her he didn't find her nearly as humorous as she found herself. "Lucy, you're testing my patience."

"Last room on the left," she murmured as she laid her head against his shoulder.

Maybe just for a few minutes she'd relax and let him care for her. This wasn't anything she'd ever had before, not even with her husband. Evan had been loving, but never the type to whisk her off her feet.

Besides, Noah wasn't doing anything but trying

to get her to rest. He wasn't trying to woo her or flirt or even seduce her.

What a shame. Part of her wished they could enter into some adult agreement that an affair was the perfect way to get each other out of their systems. Because she was seriously starting to think that she was in his, too.

The devil on one shoulder told her to be the one to seduce him, but the angel on the other told her he was grieving and to put her hormones away.

Gently, Noah laid her on her bed and eased back. "Did you already take pain meds?"

"No. I haven't been home but a few minutes." She nodded in the direction of her master bath. "In there, top shelf above the vanity."

While he got her meds, she had to admit that having him here was a bit awkward. No, maybe not awkward, but definitely weird. She couldn't deny that any man in her bedroom would make her take notice, but this particular man had her aching in places that had nothing to do with the accident.

Between that thick Southern accent and the way he obviously cared, how could she prevent her heart from flipping over?

After she took the pills, all while Noah stood directly over her to make sure, he then tucked her in like a child.

"I think I can get it from here," she informed him,

feeling more and more foolish. "Go ahead and get home. Emma is probably wondering where you are."

"She's at the sitter until this afternoon."

Well, if she were feeling up to par, she may take advantage of that fact, but as it was, she was in no shape. The longer time went on, the sorer her body was becoming. Besides, she would feel even more foolish if her first attempt at seduction landed her a big fat rejection.

"I think I need to soak in the tub first." She sat up and twisted her neck from side to side. Her hip twinged in protest, but she was careful not to show pain. "And I definitely don't need you around for that. Thanks for stopping to check on me, but I can take it from here."

"Are you seriously not going to get checked out?"

She let out a laugh and came to her feet. "I'm seriously too tired, plus I'd know if something was wrong."

Lucy wasn't going to argue. She was too sore, too tired, and not about to give in. She went past Noah and closed herself in her adjoining bathroom. This was one of those times when she was so glad she'd had an old claw foot tub put in when she'd renovated the outdated bathroom. She'd gone for an old dresser-turned-vanity, kept the old tiles, found a nice mirror at a yard sale, and splurged on the tub.

Lucy quickly shed her clothes as the tub filled with hot water. She plucked a lavender bath bomb from the basket on the vanity and dropped it into the water. If she could just get ten minutes of warmth to her muscles, she knew she'd feel better and then she could rest peacefully.

With her bath pillow in place, Lucy eased herself into the hot water that would for sure turn her skin a lovely shade of red. She didn't hear anything outside her bathroom door so she assumed Noah had left. Hopefully he remembered to lock the door behind him.

Lucy twisted her hair on top of her head and secured it with a clip. As she nestled against her little inflatable pillow, she closed her eyes and let the hot water and the bath bomb work their magic.

Maybe when she got done resting she'd feel like figuring out her car situation. Right now, though, she didn't have the mental energy to worry.

As the bubbles enveloped her, she couldn't help but get all giddy as she realized something. Despite his having worked all night and despite the fact that he needed to get home to his daughter, Noah had come to her house when he'd found out about the accident. She'd seen the worry in his eyes. He hadn't simply asked how she was while standing at her door, but had picked her up and whisked her away to bed.

She made a mental note to revise her schedule for later today. First on her agenda was figuring out exactly what that all meant.

Chapter Six

She'd been behind that closed door for so long, Noah wasn't sure if he needed to knock, call her name, or barge in to see if she was still alive.

He'd notified his sitter and explained where he was and that he may be a tad late in picking up Emma. Apparently, Emma was in no hurry to get home because they were baking cupcakes and other surprises for him.

Noah stifled a yawn and stretched his arms above his head. As tired as he was, he still hadn't calmed down from hearing Lucy had been in a hit-and-run. Maybe it was the fact he'd lost his wife tragically, or perhaps he'd been so shaken because he'd actually come to care for Lucy. Regardless, he hadn't been able to get to her house fast enough.

When he'd heard she wasn't being taken to the hospital, he'd figured she was fine, but he'd needed to see for himself. He didn't care if that was crossing some unspoken professional boundary. There was something about Lucy that stirred a desire in him, a desire he'd tried to ignore, but one that was only getting stronger.

Now that he stood in her bedroom, glancing at the pictures of her and her friends that she'd placed on her dresser, he realized just how intimate this moment was. He hadn't been in a woman's bedroom since before he was married. And suddenly he found himself in Lucy's, a woman he'd only known a short time. But in that time she'd completely taken his world for a spin. She made him fantasize, desire, ache.

Since when was that okay for a grieving man? What were the rules exactly in this situation?

Noah glanced at his watch and realized she'd been in there for nearly an hour. He crossed the room, skirting around her four-poster bed and antique trunk.

Using his knuckles, he tapped on the door. "Lucy, you all right?"

No reply. He listened, but even the sound of her swishing in the water had stopped. But how long ago?

"Lucy," he called louder in case she had earbuds in. Still nothing.

He rapped his knuckles on the door harder this

time. After a minute or so of no response or noise from the other side, he didn't even think twice. Instincts kicked in and he went for the knob. She'd been in an accident and she could've had internal injuries. What if she'd passed out? What if she'd drowned in her bathwater?

He opened the door and was met with steam. Lucy lay in the tub with her arms resting on the lip of the old claw foot bath, her head tipped to the side on one of those bath pillows. All of that blond hair had been piled up on top of her head with a few random strands clinging to her damp skin.

Noah crossed the room, wondering if she was passed out from injuries or just asleep. He crouched down next to the tub and checked for a pulse. Instantly, Lucy jerked awake. Those bright green eyes met his and his worries were put to rest as his question was answered. She'd been asleep.

And now that she was awake, he felt like a fool for standing here. All of that creamy skin was on display and it took every single ounce of his willpower to keep his eyes fixed on hers.

"Noah?" she whispered, not blinking or even attempting to cover herself.

"I thought something was wrong."

That sounded so lame, but it was the honest truth.

Lucy blinked. "I must've fallen asleep."

When she shivered, he figured the water had gotten cold since she'd come in so long ago. Noah reached for a towel and extended it to her, keeping his head turned away.

"I'm sorry for just barging in here," he stated.

Water sloshed as she must have stood up, and took the towel from him. "No. Um… I just didn't realize you were still here."

Noah turned to give her privacy, but before he could step back into the bedroom, Lucy let out a hiss in pain. He spun back to her, instantly finding his arms around her.

"I'm all right," she insisted, but she clutched his arm as she leaned into his chest. "I guess I'm a bit sorer than I thought. I just stepped wrong, that's all. My hip is not cooperating."

She'd managed to wrap the towel around her body, but she hadn't dried off. Her damp skin soaked his T-shirt, her body lined up with his perfectly, and that heaviness of guilt he'd been carrying since meeting her was growing lighter. Because holding her didn't feel so wrong after all.

Without thinking twice, he lifted her in his arms once again and carried her from the bathroom.

"Noah—"

"You're fine. I know." He went into her room and set her on the edge of her bed. "What else is hurting?"

She clutched the ends of the towel between her breasts. "Just my hip. I banged it against the door when the other car plowed into me."

Rage coiled within him at the thought of someone hurting her and fleeing the scene. Noah knew the guys were out looking for the mangled car and he hoped like hell they found the culprit.

"Go home and rest," she insisted.

Her eyes held his and he couldn't pull his gaze away from just how stunning she looked with glistening skin and honey strands framing her face.

"I'm going to rest here." He hadn't thought about that before, but he could grab some shut-eye on her couch.

"Surely there is some department rule against coworkers fraternizing."

Noah crossed his arms over his chest, his gaze never wavering from her. "Are we fraternizing?"

"Well, you've seen me naked and carried me to bed." She quirked a brow as if she had him. "The closest thing I've ever done with a coworker is have breakfast with some guys after our shift. Not one has ever been in my bedroom, let alone seen me without clothes."

Noah shrugged. "We're friends. I was worried and for good reason."

Lucy came to her feet, standing only inches from him. "My friends don't come into my bathroom when I'm taking a bath."

Why did his eyes have to go to her lips? And why did she challenge him? Couldn't she just accept his help and not be so defiant? Yet something about that independent manner turned him on.

"Get dressed," he told her. "I'm going to crash on your couch."

"Why are you so adamant about keeping an eye on me?"

There went that guilt growing back to full size. His late wife had said she was fine after the storm that ripped through their tiny town. She'd come up out of the cellar with him and Emma and kept complaining of a headache after a board had hit her in the back when they all raced to shelter.

Moments after emerging when they all thought it was safe, she collapsed and died. Just because someone said they were fine didn't mean they knew what was going on inside their bodies.

"I'll be on the sofa if you need anything," he told her.

He turned and crossed the room to the door, but her words stopped him.

"I don't know the circumstances surrounding your wife's death, but I assume that's why you're so protective now."

Noah remained in the doorway, his back to her. "You don't need to know the circumstances."

No one needed to know the details of his life before coming to Stonerock. He didn't know exactly why but it seemed imperative to maintain that privacy. He just felt that if he didn't discuss the tragedy, then the hurt might ease one day. Maybe he'd be able to leave those painful memories behind and not pull them into his new life. Hell, he had no idea. This was such unknown territory, he truly didn't know how to react.

He heard Lucy shift behind him and he stilled, waiting to see what she'd do or say. "No, I don't," she whispered. "But I know that you're still reliving that moment. You probably feel like—"

He whirled around, surprised to see she'd come so close to him and still wore only the thick terrycloth towel. "You have no idea what I feel," he growled. "Our situations aren't the same and I'm not going to let you get into my head and try to fix me."

Her bright eyes held his and he hated how terrible he felt for speaking so harshly to her. But, damn it, he wanted his thoughts, his feelings to stay locked inside where they couldn't hurt.

"I don't want to fix you," she murmured. "I want you to come to the conclusion yourself that you can be happy again."

"I'm happy."

Okay, that didn't even sound convincing to him, let alone trying to sell it to Lucy. His eyes darted over her shoulder to the picture on her bedside table. A candid shot of her and who he assumed was her late husband. After two years, the fact she still had a picture of them by her bed proved that she wasn't as far removed from grief as she'd declared.

"Since we both know you're lying," she went on, "I'd say this conversation is over."

Noah shifted his attention back to her. This woman somehow managed to frustrate him and turn him on all at the same time. One minute she challenged him, and the next she tossed out that sweetness that was so uniquely her. He never knew which Lucy he'd encounter at any given moment.

"Did you have something else to say?" she asked, still clutching that damn towel between her breasts.

"I have plenty I want to say, but this isn't the time."

When he started to turn, she grabbed his arm. "Spit it out. Don't run from whatever is on your mind."

His eyes raked over her body; he couldn't help himself at this point. She smelled too damn good, looked like something from every man's fantasy. She was killing him.

And he'd rushed over here, so there was nobody to blame but himself.

But he couldn't talk. Not now.

"You're pretty much naked and we're both exhausted," he said, as if the obvious needed to be stated. "Let's just agree to revisit this another time."

Like maybe when his head was on straight and he wasn't staring temptation right in the face.

"Revisit *this*?" she questioned. "You mean the attraction and the fact you're hiding from it?"

There she went with that no-holding-back attitude. "I'm not hiding."

"But you're attracted."

Gritting his teeth, Noah fisted his hands at his sides. There was no reason to lie about it or even attempt to deny the truth. He knew it, she knew it. The question was: What the hell did he do about it?

And why couldn't she just get dressed?

"You need to put clothes on and get some sleep," he told her.

"I plan on doing both," she informed him, tipping her head to the side. "But you don't need to stay. My hip is bruised, my back is sore, and my head hurts. I'm well past the age of needing or wanting a babysitter. And I don't take pity, either, so if that's the only reason you're hanging around—"

He kissed her. Damn it all. She was ranting and he couldn't take it another second.

Noah covered her mouth with his, but kept his fists at his side. If he reached up now, he couldn't guarantee that towel would stay in place. He'd seen exactly what she had as she lay all sprawled out in her bath and now that her body was flush against his, he had a perfect idea of how gloriously their bodies were lined up.

Lucy sighed into him and he felt her lean against him as if melting into his touch. And he desperately wanted to touch her. He hadn't kissed another woman in years, but having his mouth on Lucy wasn't a struggle and he sure as hell wasn't feeling guilty now. No, if anything he was more ramped up than ever.

When her hands settled on his shoulders and her fingers curled into him, the last shred of Noah's control snapped. He framed her face and shifted his stance, spreading his legs wider for her to step into him. She tasted so good, too good. He shouldn't be craving a woman he'd only known a short time, but there was no way he could ignore this tug.

Lucy's sweet body arched against him at the same time she let out a groan. Noah slid his hands down over her shoulders and between them to the knot in her towel. Just as he started to give it a tug, Lucy jerked and stepped back. She clutched that towel as she had before, but now she was panting...and looking anywhere but at him.

"This is..." She shook her head. "Noah, I can't."

Reality smacked him in the face and he wondered how the hell he'd gotten to this point. He'd been so adamant about not even admitting to the attraction, yet he was ready to take her to bed. And there was that picture just over Lucy's shoulder that mocked him, mocked them.

But there was something much larger going on here and it had nothing to do with the way they felt and everything to do with the fact that Lucy, who had pursued him, had pulled back and was now trembling.

Maybe she wasn't as healed as she thought.

Would he have been able to go through with this? Would he have been able to shove aside the guilt and all the reasons this was wrong and actually take her to bed?

She was right for stopping, but he wished like hell she wasn't trembling as if they'd done something wrong.

"I... I need to be alone," she whispered, still not looking his way.

Noah raked a hand through his hair. "For all your talk about wanting to heal people, did you ever stop to think you need to heal yourself first?"

She flinched at his words, but remained silent.

"I'll be at home if you need anything."

Not that she'd call. If she even spoke to him on their next shift it would be shocking. Well, spoke to him on a personal level. Because there was no way they could avoid each other forever. Communication was key to their working relationship.

And he'd just learned the hard way that they also had a personal relationship, whether either of them wanted to admit it or not. Because even though they hadn't taken things to the next level, they'd crossed an invisible line that neither of them could come back from.

Suddenly he found himself in a role reversal with the captivating Lucy Brooks. After all his mental battles with himself over keeping his pain inside, he knew he'd have to be the one to get Lucy to open up and heal because she was more broken than she'd let on…and perhaps more than she even knew.

Chapter Seven

"I figured you'd want to know."

Even as his captain spoke on the phone, Noah paid him no mind. He was too busy watching Emma play on the floor with her cowgirl doll and horse. She crawled all around the area rug chattering and pretending, looking happy and at ease. He marveled at how quickly she'd adapted to this home, this new life. Now if he could just take a page out of her book and do the same.

He could start by unloading some of those boxes stacked in his bedroom. He'd tried to make the rest of the house cozy and livable for Emma, but he hadn't brought himself to unpack the personal items they'd brought from Texas.

After the storm had torn through the town, he'd attempted to stay. He'd remained with the force and tried to rent a house and start over. But he couldn't. The few things they'd accumulated between the storm and now were still in boxes. They were just things, he told himself. His entire life had taken on a whole new perspective since that fateful day. So why hadn't he unpacked them?

When he heard the voice in his ear bark out his name, he focused his attention back on the call from his captain. "Why would I want to know this?"

Cameron laughed into the line. "I just had a hunch you'd want to know we picked up the driver who hit Lucy."

Damn it. Was he that transparent? Was something that he'd barely admitted to himself obvious to everyone else?

"Well, I'm glad he was caught," Noah stated. "Thanks for letting me know."

"I just spoke to Lucy, as well," Cameron went on to say. "She's taking the night off."

He'd been at her house earlier that day. The memories kept rolling through his mind and he'd barely slept since coming home. What little sleep he'd had had been filled with dreams of what would've happened had she not put the brakes on.

He'd woken restless, achy, needy, and cursing himself for letting things get out of hand.

Then he'd cursed himself for how far he'd let his feelings go. On one hand, he knew he couldn't grieve forever, but on the other, he felt like he was cheating on his wife.

And he honestly wasn't sure if he wouldn't have put the brakes on himself. Clearly he and Lucy weren't in a place to try to physically console each other— another reason he should seriously keep his distance. Which was easier said than done, he admitted.

"Is she okay?" Noah asked.

"Still sore and her hip is bothering her," Cameron told him. "Lucy is a hell of a worker and I'm going to hate losing her when she finishes her degree. But there are times I wish she had someone to check up on her."

"Are you meddling, sir?"

Again, Cameron's laugh filled the line. "Not at all. Just stating my opinion. Have a good day off, Spencer."

Noah disconnected the call and laid his cell on the table by the sofa. Like hell his boss wasn't meddling. But Noah knew he meant well. Happily married people always wanted to see single people happily married, too.

"Daddy, when will we have real horses again?" Emma asked, never taking her eyes off her toys. "I miss riding."

"Me, too, baby girl."

He may have been a police officer since he graduated college and the academy at the age of twenty-three, but ranching had always been his life. Their Texas ranch had been Noah's grandfather's, then his father had expanded it with more livestock and an extra barn, and once Noah had taken over, he'd grown the livestock even more.

Now he was starting from scratch. He couldn't help but wonder if this was how his grandfather had felt when he'd wanted to have his own spread and had gotten started.

This house they were renting was definitely going to be temporary because Noah needed space. He needed land.

The land Lucy had was exactly the type of space he was looking for. Something not too large so he could get started little by little.

As Noah stared down at Emma, he vowed their first purchase after the new house would be a horse. But that would take time and more funds than he had right now. He was keeping his eyes open for land to build or a house with acreage, but he wasn't going to rush. As much as he wanted all those things again, he knew it would take patience.

One day at a time. That had been his life motto since losing his world.

"I just want to ride," Emma stated again. "What if I forget how to do it?"

Noah sank into the floor beside her, smoothing a wayward strand of hair back from her face. "You won't forget. When you love something that much, it will live inside you forever."

Emma immediately looked to him. "Like Mommy? Because I never want to forget her."

Noah's heart clenched. The honest words of a child could absolutely gut you. Emma was so sincere as she stared with those bright blue eyes. Had she truly worried she'd forget her mother? Noah tried to keep pictures of her all around the house and especially one in Emma's bedroom. He wanted his late wife's memory to live on because Emma was so young, there was a good chance she'd forget the sound of her mother's voice or the way she'd laughed.

Swallowing the lump of grief, Noah pulled Emma onto his lap. "Mommy will always live in your heart, just like our ranch will. Those are things we love and just because we don't have them anymore doesn't mean we'll forget them. Moving away was just for us to start our new life. We'll have another ranch."

"And another mommy?"

Noah stilled. He'd never even thought about how Emma might think another woman would just step into their lives. At four years old, who knew how she truly viewed death? But he'd tried to explain it to her as best as he could.

Emma shifted in his lap and wrapped her arms

around his neck. "When can we go riding? Lucy said we could stop by anytime."

Noah pulled in a breath, ready to make an excuse for the "anytime" comment. But then something hit him. Lucy had called off work for the night, so she'd be awake. He wasn't sure if she was home, but if they casually dropped in, surely she wouldn't turn them away.

Yes, things had gotten out of hand earlier and she'd gotten spooked, but they couldn't hide from each other. He wasn't the type of guy to hide from confrontation, anyway. He believed in facing things head-on and trying to keep awkwardness at bay.

"Why don't you go put on your boots and we'll see if Lucy's home," he suggested. This whole plan could backfire, but he didn't think it would.

"What if she's not?" Emma asked as she scrambled off his lap.

"Then we'll go for ice cream. We need to get out of the house and have some fun."

Emma squealed and clapped her hands as she raced off to her bedroom.

Noah picked up her toys, setting them in the oversize basket next to the sofa. It was a beautiful afternoon and there was no reason he couldn't drop in on a friend.

Okay, that sounded like such a lame justification, even to his ears. He wanted to see Lucy again, plus he wanted Emma to be able to ride. Killing two birds with the same stone didn't always work, but he had a good feeling about this. Lucy wouldn't turn him away. And if she tried…well, he'd make sure she knew he was onto her. There was a deeper level of pain she didn't know she had. He'd seen the dawning come across her face earlier. When she'd pulled back, she'd appeared shocked, as if she didn't know why she had.

Things had gotten so intense, Noah knew it was time to dial it back a notch. But he couldn't walk away from her totally. No, keeping things light for a while may be exactly what they both needed.

But there was no doubt that they'd revisit what just happened. If nothing else, they needed to discuss what they were feeling, but Noah sure as hell wasn't ready for that conversation. And he definitely wasn't ready to act on that fantasy he had of Lucy.

One day at a time, right? Wasn't that his motto lately? He needed to remember that because he couldn't handle any more right now.

Lucy hadn't gone to Tammy's home to check on her, but she did call. Tammy had already heard about Lucy's accident, so they discussed that instead of the passing of her dog.

After their call, since Lucy was technically homebound, she opted to bake. She'd wanted to try out a new recipe anyway, so now was the perfect opportunity.

With the volume cranked up on the oldies she loved to listen to, Lucy tapped her foot as she worked the dough for the cranberry lemon bread. Anything fruity was her go-to. Most women loved chocolate, but Lucy would take a good lemon bar or pineapple upside-down cake over a brownie any day.

Oh, lemon bars sounded good. They were easy enough, so maybe she'd make those for Monday's meeting. She already had most of the ingredients out for the lemon cranberry bread anyway.

Singing along to the tunes, Lucy barely heard her doorbell ring. Kate and Tara had offered to take her anywhere and had even said they'd run over to keep her company, but Lucy had told them she'd be fine and her insurance was already getting her a rental car until she figured out what to do in regards to getting a new one.

She didn't dare mention to them about Noah being here earlier. She was still trying to grasp the fact he'd been willing to sleep with her and she'd all but freaked out. What was wrong with her? She hadn't been this attracted to another man since her husband.

But she hadn't been with another man, either.

After she'd flipped and put a halt to the intimacy, Noah had agreed it was a mistake. But part of her wondered if he wouldn't have stopped himself. Would he have pushed her away? Would he have let that guilt creep in and put doubts in his mind?

Lucy couldn't pinpoint exactly which emotion had caused her to stop. Being kissed by Noah was as glorious as she'd imagined it would be. Her entire body had craved more of his touch. But everything about the experience, as thrilling as it had been, seemed so unfamiliar to her. It had been too long since she'd been touched by a man and she'd been…well, terrified. Not of Noah, but of getting close to another man again.

Lucy wiped her hands on her yellow-and-white-striped apron and padded barefoot through the house. Well, more like she limped. Her hip was bothering her more than she'd initially thought it would be and the swollen, bruised area kept rubbing against her clothes. But she was lucky. In her years as a dispatcher, she'd heard of too many hit-and-runs that had ended in tragedy.

When Lucy glanced out the front window, she recognized that black truck in her drive. She hadn't emotionally recovered from when Noah was here early this morning, but she wasn't going to ignore him. And she couldn't deny the way her heart kicked up.

As much as she'd thought she was ready to move on, clearly that had not been the case. Unfortunately, she hadn't known how she'd react until she'd gotten into the moment. Now she knew and she was mortified.

Pulling in a deep breath, Lucy flicked the lock and opened the door. Noah held Emma in his arms as he met her gaze.

"We were hoping you'd be home," he said, offering a smile. "We thought we'd take you up on your offer and check out your horses."

Her horses? He'd popped in with such a simple request as if he hadn't had his hands all over her only hours ago. As if she hadn't basically shoved him out the door when her mind had overridden her feelings. He'd brought his daughter here to see the horses. Well, okay then.

"Sure. Come on in."

Lucy stepped back and let them inside. She didn't know what she expected when she saw him again, but she'd assumed it would be at work where there would be plenty of people to buffer the awkward tension between them.

As Noah passed by, Lucy inhaled that familiar deep woodsy cologne he always had on. Why did everything about this man appeal to her? Before this morning she'd relished the fact she was feeling so alive and getting to the point where she wanted to open up to those feelings of desire again.

Of course that plan had backfired because she'd rushed things, and now she probably came across as a total moron. After all, Noah was only here for Emma and the horses. There were several ranches and horse owners in Stonerock, but Noah didn't know too many people yet. Or perhaps this was his way of clearing the air and getting them back on even footing.

"Something smells good."

Lucy closed the door. "I was just mixing up some bread dough."

As she started to pass by, Noah sat Emma down and grabbed Lucy's arm. "You're limping."

That touch was so simple, yet she knew exactly how potent it was when he wanted it to be. Noah Spencer did things to her, things she hadn't experienced in years, and things she was still trying to process.

"Just sore. That's all." She wasn't about to get into all of this again, so she turned her attention to Emma who reached up to hold on to her daddy's hand. "How about you help me put the bread in the oven and then we can go check on Gunner and Hawkeye. They would love to see you."

Lucy headed down the hall to the kitchen and pulled over a chair. "Hop up here so you can see better," she told Emma. "This will go so much faster with a helper."

From the corner of her eye, Lucy noticed Noah hanging back. If he could do something else besides stare, that would be great.

Was he regretting this morning? Was he having second thoughts about kissing her and pushing toward something else? He'd been so adamant about not opening up and when he had, she'd shut him down.

She'd better be more careful about what she asked him for. Noah Spencer was one powerful man, and when he let his guard down, he was one dangerous man. Lucy could easily see herself falling for him and that was a whole other level of intimacy she truly didn't know if she was ready for.

"Can we make cookies?" Emma asked, cutting into Lucy's very adult thoughts.

Lucy laughed and reached for the greased bread pan. "Let's get this bread in the oven first and check on the horses."

"Emma," Noah chimed in, "we didn't stop by to bake."

Throwing a glance over her shoulder, Lucy met his dark gaze. "Just for the horses, right?"

Noah raised a brow as his mouth kicked up in a grin. "Right."

Every part of her tingled, from her messy hair to her pink polished toes. Perhaps it was best if they went outside. The bread could be covered and put in the oven later.

"Tell you what," she said to Emma. "Let's lay a towel over this bowl and let the bread rise awhile. That way we can enjoy the horses while it's still daylight. Once the sun goes down, we'll come back in and bake."

"Cookies, too?" Emma asked.

"Emma," Noah growled.

Lucy tapped the girl on the tip of her nose. "Cookies, too. Now let's go check out the horses. They are going to need some straw and water."

After helping Emma off the chair, Noah held the back door open and the child bounced down the steps, her curly pigtails bobbing against the sides of her head.

Lucy followed, stepping out onto the porch with Noah.

"I'll help you down the steps," he said, gripping her elbow.

Lucy didn't shrug him off, mainly because she wanted to get used to his touch. "I can hold on to the banister."

"And I can hold on to you," he claimed.

There was no need to argue. "So you're here just for the horses…or did you have a more obvious reason?"

He assisted her down the stairs, keeping that firm hold on her arm and lining his body up with hers. "I wasn't going to let this tension come between us. And I wanted to see you again. As simple and as complicated as that."

Lucy turned her gaze to his. "Is this you admitting you're interested?"

Once again his dark eyes held hers. "I think you know how much I'm interested. It was you who pushed me away this morning."

"I wasn't sure how you'd feel after I…"

Recalling the events in her mind was humiliating enough. She truly didn't want to say the words aloud.

"You think because you weren't ready that I'm suddenly not interested? I have no clue what the hell is going on here, Lucy, but I know there's an attraction I can't ignore. I can't guarantee I'm ready for more, but…"

Noah turned, one hand on each side of the bannister, blocking her from going down the steps. His eyes bore into hers.

"It took a hell of a lot of nerve for me to admit I wanted you," he finally said. "I figured if I came back with Emma, we could just start over with friendship."

Lucy nodded and realized she was still wearing her apron. She untied it and pulled it over her head, tossing it over to the porch swing.

"Friendship is a good start," she admitted, meeting his eyes once again. "You know, nothing about this is how I thought it would go when I saw you the first time."

"You thought I'd just come into your meetings and you'd fix me?" he asked.

"I thought you'd at least talk to me that first night instead of running away." Lucy opted to go for the full truth. "And I never thought I'd get closer to you and then not be able to— Never mind. The point is I was attracted to you from the second I saw you, but then you ran away."

Noah quirked that dark brow again. "Maybe I ran because you stood in the rain wearing a shirt that was plastered to your curves and I was getting away from temptation."

Stunned, Lucy didn't know what to say. She didn't get the chance to say anything, because Noah suddenly turned to his daughter. He walked up beside Emma where she stood at the fence, and pointed at the horses out into the field as he leaned in and told her something that made her laugh. Lucy had no clue what he was saying; she was still stuck on the declaration he'd just delivered to her.

From the beginning he'd been attracted to her and had been fighting it. Now their roles were reversed and she was wondering how they'd come this far, this fast. Maybe because she hadn't had someone in so long, hadn't experienced such emotions in years, she'd gotten wrapped up without thinking things through.

Watching Noah and Emma standing at the edge of the fence, Lucy swallowed that lump in her throat. When she and Evan had bought this house, this land, they'd agreed to fill it with children. That dream had died with him, or so she'd thought. Lucy wasn't jumping to the point of thinking she and Noah were going to grow old together, but seeing him and Emma here did give her hope. She could have the dream she'd once held on to. All she had to do was let go of that fear of getting too close and suffering such heartache again.

Wouldn't Evan have wanted her to find happiness?

One day she would. Lucy vowed to slowly approach this relationship with Noah. Because she simply couldn't afford for her heart to be broken again.

Chapter Eight

"My horse's name was Daisy."

Emma brushed the horse with circular strokes as she chatted with Lucy in the corral. Noah watched them from the fence. He knew she missed Daisy. Hell, they both missed the meager amount of livestock, but the ones that hadn't died in the storm, he'd had to sell to help with the move.

"She was a chestnut mare," Emma went on. "She loved apples."

Noah knew Emma missed that horse something fierce. Daisy had been so gentle and so perfect for Emma. Their daily routine of feeding her apples in the evening was no more. Soon, though, they would start new traditions in this new town. They were slowly rebuilding their lives.

"Animals are like family," Lucy added as she leaned her arm on the fence post. "These were my husband's horses and I'd thought about selling them when he passed away, but I wanted to hold on to them as a way to stay connected to him. I'm glad I decided to keep them."

Noah knew that need to hold on to any aspect of a late spouse, but everything he'd had with his wife had been taken. Except for Emma. And at the end of the day, that's all he needed.

"Daddy says Mommy will always live in my heart."

Noah glanced to Emma, who was looking back at him. He shot her a wink and she smiled. Yeah, they had each other and that's all that mattered. Memories would live on as long as he had any say about it.

"That's true," Lucy agreed. "Once you love someone, they will stay with you forever. My husband will always be in my heart as well. Being sad is okay, but we also deserve to be happy."

"I think that's solid advice," Noah stated as he turned his focus to Lucy. When she quirked a brow, he merely grinned.

"Daddy says we'll get another horse soon, but first we have to find a house that has enough land." Emma set the brush back in the bucket. "I think I'll name my new horse Daisy. I really like that name."

"Nothing wrong with that," Lucy stated with a firm nod. "But you can come over here anytime to ride or to just see these guys. They love company and I can always use help." Because of her sore hip, today was not a good day to ride.

The sun stretched an orange glow across the horizon and Noah pushed off the fence. "Maybe we should let Lucy get back to what she was doing before we came."

"I was baking, which I promised Emma could help me with." Lucy opened the gate and unhooked Gunner's reins from the post. "Let me get him put up and we'll go back inside."

"We don't need to take up your entire day," Noah argued. "I didn't expect you to have her help."

"Well, I made a promise," Lucy told him as she threw a look over her shoulder. "I never go back on a promise, especially since I've been thinking of cookies ever since Emma mentioned them."

Emma drew lines in the dirt with the toe of her boot. She didn't seem to be paying much attention and had gone to wherever her four-year-old mind journeyed from time to time.

"Are you sure?" Noah asked Lucy as she came back and closed the gate.

Resting her arm over the rung, she nodded. "Positive. If you have something else to do, go on ahead. Emma and I will get along just fine. We'll have a little girl time and you can go do…whatever it is you want."

"Is this you trying to push me away again?"

Lucy pursed her lips and tipped her head. "I'm just trying to figure all of this out. Besides, kids are honest, so I'll quiz her and we'll see just how interested in me you really are."

Noah laughed. "Fair enough. But I really don't have anything else to do."

"I'm sure you'll think of something." Lucy turned her attention to Emma. "You up for some girl time if we kick Daddy out for a few hours?"

Emma glanced up, her eyes darting to her father. "Is that okay? Lucy's fun and I really want to make cookies, Daddy."

Lucy stared at Noah as if daring him to argue with two females. He wasn't that stupid. Besides, giving Emma a little female bonding time was probably a great idea. Perhaps it would do them both good and Noah could use the time to figure out what the hell kind of emotional roller coaster he was on.

Noah threw his hands up. "Fine, but I want some of those cookies you guys keep talking about."

"Promise," Emma said as she drew an invisible X over her heart.

Noah had no idea what he'd do. Seriously. For the past six months he'd been with Emma or at work. He didn't have hobbies and there was no ranch to occupy his time, so…what the hell should he do?

"You're still here," Lucy stated. "It's difficult to have girl time when you won't go."

Emma giggled and Noah leaned down and smacked a kiss on her forehead. "I'm going. You have my cell, so if you need anything—"

"We won't," Lucy assured him. "Give us two hours."

There weren't many people he'd trust his little girl with, but he definitely trusted Lucy. Hell, he'd trusted her so much he was ready to sleep with her.

As he headed to his truck, he wondered where he should go. There weren't too many options in this small town. Maybe he'd just go to the local bar. It wasn't but a couple miles away on the main drag and he'd been meaning to swing by there. He'd heard they had really good burgers and he could use some time to himself to think.

Emma was growing pretty fond of Lucy…and Noah couldn't deny he was, too.

One day at a time. Looking too much into this or placing too much hope in one situation was just asking for heartache—something he couldn't afford.

"Need a beer?"

Yeah, he did. About six of them. "I'll just stick with soda."

The bartender turned to grab a glass and fill it with ice. "You're the new officer."

Small towns, Noah thought. Gotta love them.

"Noah Spencer," he said, offering his hand for a

shake. More than likely the bartender knew this, but it was still polite to start with introductions. "This is the first chance I've had to stop in here, but I've heard all about the burgers."

"Best in town." With his free hand he slid the glass of soda across the bar. "Gray Gallagher."

Noah gripped the glass. "The owner?"

Gray propped his hands on the bar. "Third generation."

"No kidding."

Gray nodded, resting his hands on the gleaming bar top. "My grandfather opened this bar when he returned from the war, then my father went into the Marines and he took over when he got out. I took over when I came home from the Army."

Impressed, Noah nodded. "You've got quite a family tradition."

"Minus the difference in military fields." Gray smiled. "We've had a few disagreements over which is the best."

Gray started to say something else, but glanced over Noah's shoulder. The man's lips thinned and a flash of something—jealousy maybe—came and went across his face.

Noah glanced over his shoulder to see a beautiful blonde fast-dancing with a group of guys. Harmless, flirty fun from the looks of things, but Gray didn't seem too keen on this.

"Problem?"

Gray pulled in a deep breath. "Just since high school."

Definitely jealousy. Noah didn't know what that emotion felt like, but from the looks of Gray, Noah didn't want to know.

"Hang on a second."

Gray disappeared, and Noah thought for sure he'd be heading across that wooden dance floor to interfere, but he didn't. Gray ended up at the other end of the bar, leaning over to talk to a guy who sat by himself nursing a bottle. From the looks of things, the customer was drowning his sorrows. If only life were that easy. Unfortunately, getting lost in the bottle didn't fix anything and reality was always waiting for you on the other side.

Noah glanced over the menu and quickly chose the loaded garbage burger. Anything that combined a burger with bacon, onion rings and barbecue sauce was for him. Sign him up. The messier the better.

"Sorry about that," Gray said as he came back. He nodded toward the menu. "Decide what you want?"

Noah placed his order and pulled his phone from his jacket pocket. He'd apparently had it on vibrate and had missed some texts from Lucy. Worried something was wrong, he opened the messages. Clearly there was no need to worry because his daughter was having a blast.

One picture had Emma wearing a huge apron tied in knots around her waist and neck. She was holding her hands up, palms out to show all the dough she'd been mixing. He scrolled down to see another, this time a selfie with Emma and Lucy, wide smiles across their faces.

His heart flipped in that second. There were two wounded souls bonding and living in the moment. They were virtual strangers, yet they appeared to be having the time of their lives. And Noah couldn't deny that attraction he'd initially had for Lucy grew even more. Something was happening here—nothing he was ready to put a label on quite yet, but definitely something more than just friendship.

How could that be? He wasn't ready for more... was he?

Noah scrolled on to some action shots of Emma kneading the dough and forming it in the bread pans, then the last photo of her holding up a bag of chocolate chips. Obviously cookies were next. There were many things Noah could do with Emma, but baking was definitely not his area of expertise.

The music in the bar switched from fast-paced to something slow and sultry. Noah took a drink of his soda and glanced around. The woman Gray had been eyeing earlier now danced with one guy, her arms draped lazily around his neck. Noah figured in this small town, he'd hear the gossip soon enough about that pretty blonde. Funny how her short skirt and plaid shirt tied at the waist did nothing for him, but the headstrong dispatcher who dressed on the conservative side did more than he should allow.

A waitress came with his burger and fries and set the plate next to his drink. "Can I get you anything else?"

"This will be fine. Thanks."

He sent off a text to Lucy informing her he'd be back within the hour. Maybe he'd get to sample the baked goods.

The commotion behind him caught Noah's attention. He hadn't even tasted his burger yet before he was off his stool. Gray was standing between the blonde and the guy she'd been dancing with. The blonde didn't look happy, neither did Gray, and the other guy was yelling something about Gray minding his own business.

Noah quickly crossed the scarred floor. "Problem?"

Gray kept his grip on the guy's shirt. "Just taking out the garbage."

"I can handle myself," the lady argued.

The guy in the strangle hold gripped Gray's wrists. "She shouldn't dress like that."

Gray's face literally turned red as he reared back with a closed fist. Noah jumped in just in time, but managed to take the brunt of that fist on his jaw. He shoved the other guy out of the way, someone screamed, and Noah held both of his arms out. Keeping these two guys from fighting was key, not the fact his jaw was throbbing.

"Damn, man. You all right?" Gray asked.

Noah shot him a glance. "Maybe you need to go in the back and cool off. I'll take care of things here."

Gray glared at the other guy.

"Now, Gallagher," Noah demanded.

Gray turned to the woman and she merely shook her head and went back to her table of friends. Now that Noah was close, he recognized her as one of Lucy's friends from the meeting that first night.

Whatever the story was, he was sure he'd hear it because he was going to go have a detailed get-to-know-you meeting with Gray Gallagher very shortly.

Once Gray left them, Noah turned to the other guy. "What happened?"

"He tried to punch me."

Noah wasn't in the mood. He had a burger waiting on him and he highly doubted Gray would've just sabotaged his business and threatened a patron for no reason. Yes, a woman was a valid motivation for a man to get fired up over, but Noah figured he would've heard about issues with Gallagher's if a bar fight was a normal occurrence.

"What did you do to her?" Noah asked, thumbing over his shoulder toward Lucy's friend.

Of course the guy said nothing, but kept his eyes level with Noah in an arrogant expression.

"Now would be a good time for you to go."

The guy snorted. "And who the hell are you?"

"Officer Spencer, Stonerock PD." He waited a beat. "Any more questions?"

The guy glanced to where Lucy's friend sat, then back to Noah. "She's not worth it."

"She's worth more, so get the hell out of here."

Muttering a string of curses, the guy headed out of the bar.

Once he'd left, Noah crossed to the table of ladies. "Everything all right here?"

Lucy's friend stared up at him with wide brown eyes. She flashed him a smile that no doubt had many men bowing to her commands. He felt nothing.

"I'm fine." She extended her hand. "We haven't been properly introduced. I'm Kate McCoy."

Noah shook her hand. "Noah Spencer."

"I've heard about you from Lucy."

Fantastic. Just what he wanted to be part of. Girl gossip.

"I'm Tara Bailey." Noah shifted his attention to the raven-haired beauty across the booth. He recognized her from the meeting, too. "I figured Lucy was with you since we invited her out tonight and she turned us down. She never turns us down."

They figured she was with him? Just what did that mean? No way was he about to tell them she was with his daughter. That would only add more fodder to the rumor mill. With him being new to town, he was trying like hell to stay off the radar. Plus, being an officer of the law, he prided himself on privacy. Clearly he was failing on both counts.

"I'm just here for the burgers," he replied, ready to be done here. "Have a good evening, ladies."

As he headed back to his vacated stool, he wondered if he should get his food to go so he could get back to Lucy and Emma. Then he noticed Gray standing on the other side of the counter.

"Sorry about that." The bartender gestured toward Noah's jaw. "You going to arrest me for clocking you?"

Noah shook his head. "If I thought you meant it for me, you'd already be at the station."

Gray gave a clipped nod. "The burger is on the house."

Noah laughed. "I'd rather pay for my food." He rubbed his jaw. "You have a mean hook."

Gray eyed the side of Noah's face and Noah was confident there was a bruise because he knew it was swollen. "How about some ice?"

"I'll take care of it when I get home." Noah took a seat on the stool and rested his elbows on the bar. "Care to tell me what set you off, other than that guy was a jerk?"

The muscle in Gray's jaw ticked. "I saw his hands moving toward the hem of her skirt and she shoved him. Then he grabbed her and hauled her against him and I lost it."

"Before you lost it, was she aware how you feel about her?"

Gray laughed and shook his head. "We have a history."

"Were you married?"

"Hell no," Gray declared. "We've been best friends since high school. Lucy, Tara, Kate and me. We grew apart when I went off to the Army, but since I've been back, we've reconnected. They come in here pretty often, but Tara and Lucy don't push my buttons the way Kate does. It's like she knows exactly how to irritate me."

Noah figured he may as well eat while his food was somewhat still warm. "She's taunting you," he stated as he picked up his burger. "None of my business. Just offering my unsolicited opinion."

He took a bite and nearly groaned. This was the best burger he'd ever had. No wonder the place was so popular.

"Oh, she's taunting me, all right." A waitress came to the bar with an order and Gray grabbed two frosted mugs and filled them with beer before passing them over. "She knows how I feel and it's like she thrives on it."

"Have you dated other women?" Noah asked. "I mean, maybe you should and see if that helps you get over her or makes her realize that she likes you."

Gray raked a hand through his hair. "I'm the bar

owner. I give advice and opinions to my customers. Not the other way around."

"Yeah, well, I'm sure you'll get your chance with me," Noah replied as he picked up a chip. "I'm the new guy in town and I'm sure you've heard all about my life."

"Heard you had a tough time in Texas. Sorry about your loss, man."

Noah nodded. "Thanks. It's hell trying to move on, but there's little choice when you have a child looking to you for guidance and stability."

"We all carry our own hell," Gray muttered as he glanced to the guy at the end of the bar.

"What's his story?" Noah asked.

Keeping his eyes on the guy toying with his beer bottle, Gray replied, "That's Sam Bailey."

Bailey... Bailey. "Isn't that the same last name as the lady over there with Kate?"

"Tara is Sam's ex-wife. They've been divorced for a year. That's a mess. Hell, *he's* a mess."

Obviously. "So why is he here if she's here?"

Gray grabbed a rag from beneath the counter and started wiping off the pass-through where the waitresses came for drinks. "He comes here all the time for dinner and tends to stick around to talk to me. I think he hates being home, if I'm being honest. He kept the house in the divorce. They have a five-year-old little girl. Sam just told me she's at his mom's tonight for a sleepover."

Noah glanced to the man at the end of the bar. He had no idea what the circumstances were surrounding the divorce, but Noah knew the heartache of losing your wife, the empty feeling you couldn't fill. But he had no idea what hell existed when you lost your wife but still saw her frequently.

Noah finished his meal as Gray went about filling drink orders and randomly talking to Sam. This town was proving to be more and more interesting. No doubt Gray had seen it all.

As Noah threw a tip on the bar, he called to Gray, "Stay out of trouble."

"What trouble?" Gray asked with a side grin.

Noah headed out the door and figured he'd make his way back to Lucy's, grab some cookies and Emma, then go on home to ice his jaw. In some ridiculously warped way, he almost felt like that was some male bonding experience between Gray and himself. It had been a long time since he'd been blindsided by a blow like that. But if that kept Gray from punching someone else and risking the reputation of his business, then Noah would sacrifice his face.

Noah hoped Gray got his head on straight where Kate was concerned, though. Noah didn't intend on lending the other side of his jaw next time.

Chapter Nine

Lucy was putting the cookies in a tin for Emma to take home when the back door opened. She smiled that he was so comfortable to walk in without knocking.

"Just in t—"

Anything she was about to say vanished the second she saw Noah's face. Cookies forgotten, she stepped forward. She reached out to touch his jaw, but realized he must be hurting. Her hand landed on his shoulder instead.

"What happened?"

Noah smiled. Actually smiled as he shook his head. "It's nothing. My face got in the way."

"Daddy, are you okay?"

Emma scrambled off the bar stool and came over to stand between Lucy and Noah.

"I'm fine, sweetheart," he assured her. "It smells amazing in here. I hope you made something we can take home."

Emma nodded, but Lucy couldn't take her eyes off the blue-and-purple swollen jaw. Noah threw her a glance that silently told her he'd talk about it later.

Pulling in a breath, Lucy nodded and went to finish putting bread and cookies in containers for them to take home. Her kitchen was an absolute disaster, but she didn't care.

Tara and Kate were likely at Gallagher's dancing but Lucy knew she couldn't have had more fun if she'd gone with them. It wasn't like she had ever spent the evening with a toddler, but she'd quickly found that she was having a blast staying in for a change and being silly, tossing flour at each other, cracking eggs, and having shells fall into the cookie batter. Each mishap caused Emma to laugh even louder so Lucy found herself purposely doing things wrong.

Emma spoke of her mother, she spoke of the ranch in Texas, and how she and her daddy always worked together in the evenings when he came home from the police station. She said he'd helped keep bad people off the streets in Texas and he was going to do the same here. She wished he didn't work at night, but Lucy had explained that because he was new, that was the only shift available.

It must be difficult being a single father and at the mercy of your employment, but Noah hadn't complained to her or anyone else that she'd noticed. He did his job, cared for his daughter…and managed to melt Lucy's heart in the process.

Fantastic. Now she was falling for a guy that she couldn't even bring herself to be intimate with. It had been two years since Evan passed. He would've wanted her to move on, and she truly thought she was ready. At least her body had been more than ready, but her mind and heart started battling and she'd shut down.

Lucy set the tins on the island. "Emma, would you like to go in and finish watching that movie I put on earlier?"

Emma looked to her dad. "Is it okay?"

He nodded. "You can go."

As Emma raced into the living room, Lucy explained, "I hope it was okay I started a movie while everything was baking. She said you watch it at home, so I figured it was safe."

Noah nodded. "I trust your judgment."

Lucy eyed his face, hating he'd been hurt. "Ready to tell me what happened to you?"

"I met Gray Gallagher."

Stunned, Lucy gasped. "Gray hit you? Why?"

"Your friend Kate frustrates him and she likes to push his buttons."

A sliver of jealousy speared her. Lucy knew how

Kate acted around attractive men. She was like a magnet and they seemed to gravitate toward her. No doubt Noah was just like all the other guys who found Kate irresistible.

"You were flirting with Kate?"

"What? No," he said. "She was dancing with some guy. Apparently Gray saw the guy get a little too handsy and charged after him. I tried to stop it. Well, I did stop it."

Lucy tipped her head as she reached out, barely brushing her fingertip over the bruise. "I'm sorry you got hurt. Want some ice or pain reliever?"

The muscle beneath her finger clenched and she glanced up to his eyes. His lids were lowered, but the dark eyes staring back at her held nothing but desire, want. Her heart picked up and the knots in her stomach clenched. No matter how many times she told herself to take this slow with him, some things were simply out of her control.

"It's suddenly feeling better," he rasped.

Lucy flattened her palm against his cheek, still careful not to put too much pressure on the swollen area. "Gray really is a nice guy. He and Kate… they're complicated."

"More complicated than us?"

Us. Well, he'd thrown that gauntlet down and the word solidified something…didn't it?

Kate and Gray were meant for each other, though Kate was frustrating and Gray was stubborn. The two never could see eye to eye on anything other than the fact that they both irritated each other. But anyone could see how the sparks would fly whenever they were in close proximity.

When Lucy was around Noah, they didn't so much irritate each other as confuse each other. The need, the guilt, the fear of moving forward all combined to make their situation so complex.

"Not the same," she corrected. "But just as confusing."

He nodded, then looked at her, his expression serious. "I'm sorry I let things get out of hand this morning."

Was that just this morning? The day seemed so long. So much had happened since the encounter in her bedroom.

"We're both to blame for that," she told him as she dropped her hand. "But I should apologize for freaking out. I just… I never thought that would be an issue."

"I never thought I'd want another woman," he countered. "I *can't* want another woman. It's too soon."

He seemed to be telling himself rather than her.

Lucy couldn't stop looking at those mesmerizing eyes and how they seemed to see right into her soul. How could a man be this expressive with his emotions and not be ready?

Granted she thought she could move on, but fear had her rethinking that theory.

They were at different points in their grieving and Lucy didn't want to get hurt again—and she certainly didn't want to hurt him, either.

Lucy crossed her arms over her chest so she didn't reach back out to him. "Neither of us can afford more heartache."

Noah nodded in agreement. "I have a daughter to protect."

There went more of that melting heart. "What about your needs, Noah?"

"She's my world," he said with a shrug. "There's nothing I wouldn't do for her and that includes putting all of my needs last."

Her eyes drifted to his jaw once again and she couldn't help but wonder about the details of the evening. What happened when he'd first gone into Gallagher's, how he and Gray had ended up striking up a conversation, and how Noah's face had ultimately landed between Gray's fist and some guy.

"You didn't tell anyone that we were…"

How did she ask properly without sounding like she was embarrassed?

"I mean, if my friends thought I was here with Emma, they'd think more…"

"I get it." Noah ran a hand over the uninjured side of his face, the stubble along his jawline bristling beneath his palm. "Nobody needs to know how good of friends we are. They'll only read more into it."

Good friends? Considering he'd seen her completely naked and he'd kissed her enough to spawn fantasies for days, she'd say they were extremely good friends.

"Well, Kate and Tara know a little."

Noah's mouth kicked up in a side grin. "I figured, but I just need to keep Emma protected, and for the sake of my job, I don't want any rumors circulating at work."

"You're getting nothing but praise at work lately, especially after saving that little boy."

Noah shook his head and dropped his arms. "I just happened to be the one to see him, that's all."

"You split up a would-be fight at Gallagher's and you're sporting a wound to prove it, so you may get more praise."

Noah laughed. "I think as angry and jealous as Gray was, he would've kicked that guy's ass as he shoved him out the door. It wouldn't have been much of a fight."

The television from the living room seemed to get even louder just before Emma let out a string of chuckles.

"That's her favorite part," Noah said with a laugh. "We watch that movie over and over."

"As soon as the cookies went in the oven she asked if I'd ever seen it."

Noah smiled, showcasing that dimple that drove her mad. "I think even more so now that we moved, she wants that connection. The horses in the film remind her of Daisy."

Lucy's heart ached for the precious child who had lost her mother and her beloved horse.

"In case nobody has told you, you're doing a phenomenal job."

Noah's brows drew in. "At what?"

With a shrug, Lucy replied, "Life. My husband passed away, too. I know the pain, the emptiness. I get that you don't know which way to turn for happiness or if it even exists anymore."

She didn't want to get too far into that part of her life, but she wanted him to know how much she understood, how she could offer support.

"I know after Evan passed, I went into this depression. I had survivor's guilt even though I wasn't there when he died. I was questioning why I had the opportunity to move on and be happy when he didn't. If it weren't for my friends, I'm not sure where I'd be. If you want to talk…"

He scratched the side of his jaw. "It's the hardest thing I've ever dealt with in my life," he admitted. "There are days I don't want to get out of bed. There are times, more often than not, that the survivor's guilt threatens to take over. But Emma needs her father at one hundred percent because right now, I'm mom and dad to her."

The lump in Lucy's throat seemed to grow with each raw word of honesty. "I'm here if you need a sounding board," she said. "As a friend, I know. But it's important to get that adult time and communication during your grieving process."

"I'm pretty sure my shrink in Texas gave me all the adult time I could need for the rest of my life." Noah reached over and slid the tins toward the edge of the counter. "I better get going. Thanks for having Emma over to see the horses and to bake."

"You guys are welcome here anytime." Lucy knew the night had to come to an end, but she hated for him to go. "I liked having her around. And you."

"Glad to hear it."

She opted to push a little more, testing both their comfort zones. "When we're off again, maybe you two can come back for horse riding and a picnic."

Noah eased back, his eyes holding hers. "Count on it."

"Are you sure you don't want ice for your jaw?" Lucy hated the thought of her friend losing his cool and hitting Noah.

"Nah. I've had worse," he told her. "I'll put something on it when I get home. How's the hip?"

"I've had so much fun this evening, I've forgotten about it," she admitted. "It hurts more when I walk on it, but I think that's also going to help work out the soreness."

Noah stared at her another minute and Lucy had no idea what was running through his mind. He kept his eyes on her, but said nothing. The silence stretched between them with only the faint sound of the television in the background.

"Thank you," he finally said, his voice full of emotion. "There's not much lately that really penetrates the hurt, but you have. You've not only been great for me, but to spend this time with Emma... I can't thank you enough. I know she misses having a female in her life. Her sitter is great, but someone younger and fun is what she needed for a night."

Lucy placed her hand on his. "She's precious. I can be a friend to you both."

"All while juggling work, your community service and your schoolwork?" Noah reached up with his free hand and smoothed the stray strands off her forehead. "Who takes care of you?"

"I don't need anyone to take care of me."

Though having him touch her was something she wasn't about to turn down. At least, touching when it was innocent and simple. Anything else, well, she'd have to work up to that. But Noah was the first man in so long she even wanted to explore that notion with, so she'd keep moving along and hoping something blossomed from this, because Noah Spencer was one special guy. And his daughter had captured Lucy's heart, as well.

Now she had to figure out where to put all these feelings and how to sort them.

"Maybe you could come to the next meeting?" Lucy suggested.

Noah shook his head. "I don't need meetings. I'm getting along without them."

She wished he'd just come to one, to see that it wasn't all doom and gloom. People needed a support team, and while Noah had Emma, how could the man actually grieve when he had to be so strong for a child?

"Maybe you'll reconsider," she added.

Noah's dark eyes held hers. "Don't try to get into my head, Lucy. I'm going at my own pace and it's nobody's business but mine."

He headed into the living room, clearly done with the topic. How could they move forward if he wasn't prepared to face his pain?

Lucy sank to a kitchen bar stool as her own hurt spiraled through her. Perhaps he didn't want to move forward. He'd apologized for the kiss; he'd made it clear they could be friends. He'd summed up everything neat and tidy. But Lucy didn't feel the discussion of their situation was closed. Not by a long shot.

Chapter Ten

"Why don't you put the tray of cookies over on that table against the wall?" Lucy suggested.

Tara rolled her eyes and Kate snorted. They'd both just come in the back door and Lucy was already in a panic because the community center wasn't nearly ready for the Helping Hands open house. Why were they just standing there?

"What?" Lucy asked.

"You think we can just come in here and set up for the open house and we're not going to address the fact that Noah was in Gallagher's and did some male bonding with Gray?"

"By bonding, do you mean fighting?" Lucy countered. "Because I saw his face afterward."

Kate's eyes widened. "He came to your house after? Did you make him forget all about his troubles?"

Lucy picked up the tray and crossed the room. "I'm not discussing this with you two."

"Why not?" Tara asked. "I'm sure you heard all about Gray losing his cool over Kate, and Sam nursing a beer all night."

Lucy set the tray down and turned to face her friends. "Actually, I hadn't heard about Sam at all. And I only got the abridged version of Gray."

The fact Sam was nursing a beer at Gray's bar wasn't exactly news. For the past year he'd been somewhat depressed and Gray always had his back. Lucy wished Sam and Tara would make up, for the sake of their daughter for one reason. But she knew that not every marriage was meant to be.

"Why do you two keep going there?" Lucy insisted, more than happy to turn the topic to her friends. "Why taunt those men?"

"Sam isn't always there," Tara defended. "And when he is, he hugs the same bottle all night, so I know he's not drunk. He doesn't even look my way."

But Sam knew full well his ex-wife was there dancing and having a good time. And Sam didn't look her way because it hurt to see her. Anybody could understand his logic. It wasn't just death that caused people to grieve.

"What's your excuse?" Lucy asked Kate. "You know Gray has been half in love with you for years."

Kate shrugged and smoothed her hands down her simple tunic. "He's not in love with me or halfway there. He just sees me as a challenge." She shrugged. "It's not worth damaging our friendship to let him have his thrills."

Lucy understood that logic, but at the same time, she truly believed Gray loved Kate. Maybe one of these days Kate would realize it, too.

"Let's get back to you," Tara suggested. "Noah is one hot guy. I hadn't gotten a good look at him until he came over to our table last night."

Lucy rolled her eyes. "We don't have time for adolescent girl talk. We have people coming in thirty minutes and nothing is set up the way it should be."

Kate, sarcastic as ever, pointed to the tray. "You just put those cookies in place."

Pulling in a deep breath and attempting some sort of control, Lucy addressed her friends. "Let me make this brief. Noah and I are friends. He's new on the force and is still making an impression. He has a child to look out for who just lost her mother six months ago. Rumors aren't something he can afford right now. So let's get the chairs moved out of the way so people can mingle, and get the new pamphlets on all of the tables so people don't have to hunt for them. We also need to get the music going so it's not so quiet and awkward when the first guests arrive."

Kate and Tara exchanged a look, but Lucy was done with the grilling of her social life. How could she explain it when she truly had no idea herself what was going on with Noah Spencer? And, as much as she loved her friends, she also wanted to keep Noah to herself.

Lucy ignored Tara and Kate's quizzical stares and circled around them to start setting up. They were expecting quite the crowd this evening. Their flyers had been up all over Stonerock for the past month. Their regular attendees had invited friends and family. They were hoping to spread the word that everyone could benefit from Helping Hands. If someone wasn't going through a rough patch now, it might only be a matter of time. As depressing as that sounded, it was the reality. Everyone would experience loss at least once in their lives.

The main point of tonight was to see if there was a greater need. The loss of a family member or friend wasn't the only thing that people grieved over. Sometimes it was the breakup of a marriage, the loss of a job, depression, anxiety. There was a host of problems people dealt with on a day-to-day basis, and Lucy didn't want people to feel alone in their struggles.

She'd invited Noah, but he hadn't acted like he'd make it. As much as he flirted and pretended to be fine, Lucy knew there was hurt just beneath the surface. He didn't talk about his wife's death at all, which only proved that speaking about it was too rough. And all of that was understandable because everyone moved at the pace that was comfortable for them. But at the same time, she truly wished he'd quit being so strong for everyone around him. They were friends—a little more than friends, if she were being totally honest—and she wanted him to trust her with his feelings.

As the first guests started to arrive, Kate, Tara, and Lucy greeted them. With a town as small as Stonerock, pretty much everybody knew everybody. Still, there may be some who brought friends from neighboring towns and Lucy wanted to make sure nobody felt left out. Wasn't that the whole point of this group?

With the holidays only a few months away, it was important now more than ever to have support.

The St. John brothers came through with their wives and children. The dynamic family was a powerhouse in this town. Cameron was her boss, so she knew him well. His brothers were known because of their wild sides as teens and now for their involvement with the town.

Eli St. John was the town doctor, having taken over after his father retired. Their brother Drake was the chief for Stonerock's fire department. They were one dynamic family in the small community.

Kate and Tara greeted the crew as Lucy refilled the coffee carafe. Lucy hoped this was a success in bringing hope to those who were struggling with loss, no matter how minor.

"This is wonderful."

Lucy turned to see Tammy standing there with a wide smile on her face. "Thank you. I think it's a great turnout."

"I wanted to introduce you to my nephew, Todd. He lost his fiancée a year ago."

The thirty-something man stepped closer to his aunt. "Pleasure to meet you."

"I'm glad you could come out," Lucy stated as she shook his hand. "You're not from Stonerock?"

"I'm actually moving here soon. I'm from Nashville."

Tammy patted Lucy on the arm. "I told Todd all about how you started this group and what a wonderful woman you are. I thought with him moving here soon, he may need a friend."

Lucy saw exactly where this was going. This wasn't the first time some well-meaning soul had tried to hook Lucy up with a family member.

"I'm sure you'll fit right in here," Lucy told him, dodging the obvious setup. "If you'll excuse me, I see some other guests I need to talk to."

"Maybe we can talk later," Todd added before she could escape.

Lucy merely smiled. "Thank you both for coming. Tara, Kate, and I are here if you need anything."

Okay, that kept things focused on the group. Lucy had never gone for being set up on a date. She'd been too busy with her job, her schooling and making sure

Helping Hands served its purpose. She hadn't even had the desire to date or even flirt with another man.

And then Noah Spencer had stepped into the back of the meeting with that black cowboy hat tipped low. A man with that type of presence, all menacing and mysterious, begged for attention. Her stomach knotted in a ball at the mere thought of him. That giddiness seemed to grow the more she was with him and the closer they became.

Lucy attempted to push aside her thoughts of Noah, though he always hovered near the forefront of her mind. She spoke with many people she recognized and met some new folks who were thinking of joining the group.

As the evening wore on, she couldn't help but glance around to see if Noah decided to make an appearance. He never did. She'd be lying if she didn't admit disappointment. Not that she thought he'd come for himself, but she'd hoped he'd come for her.

After all, they were friends, right?

Perhaps she was asking too much. They weren't actually a couple or anything, so there were no expectations…only hope.

After everyone had gone and Tara, Kate and Lucy had cleaned up, Lucy headed out the back door to her car. Darkness had set in, but the community center parking lot was well lit with halogen street lamps.

Movement to her right had her jumping, until she saw that it was Todd, the man she'd met earlier. He'd been sitting on the bench between the community center and the entrance to the park.

"I didn't mean to startle you," he stated.

He kept his distance, which helped because it was a little odd that he was out here waiting on her.

"It's fine." But still creepy, she silently admitted.

"My aunt obviously tried to play matchmaker and I wanted to apologize if you were uncomfortable."

Lucy relaxed a little more. "Oh, it's fine. I've been the target for many matchmakers."

"She means well," he added, shoving his hands into his pockets. "That being said, I wouldn't mind taking you out when I get into town. If you're free, that is."

Todd was a handsome man, he seemed to be polite and Lucy adored his aunt. But—there was of course a but—she just wasn't feeling anything toward him. Nothing at all in comparison to what she felt when Noah was near.

"Don't answer now," he went on when the silence stretched between them. "I'll look you up when I get into town permanently."

Lucy simply nodded and smiled as she headed on to her car. Todd turned toward the truck parked in the distance and pulled out of the lot. Even if Lucy were interested in Todd, she didn't feel right about going out with him, not with the way Noah occupied her mind so much lately.

As Lucy pulled in her driveway minutes later, her text alerts went off from Tara.

Turning down a date with another potential new guy? Sounds like Noah is more serious than you let on.

So what? Lucy wasn't even going to reply. No need to add fuel to the fire of her friend's comments. They may be true, but Lucy didn't have to acknowledge them.

Grabbing her purse and cell, she headed inside. She was due at work in a while and she wanted to go in and just relax until she had to leave again. She wasn't positive, but she thought Noah was off tonight. Sometimes those nights dragged because she'd gotten used to hearing his voice over the radio. But when he wasn't there, she could think. She could try to figure out just what she wanted and where she thought this relationship would go.

Because there was only so long she would want to stay in the friend category. And when she was ready to move forward, she hoped like hell he would be, too.

Chapter Eleven

"I'm five blocks away," Noah reported into the radio.

"I'm pulling in now," another officer responded.

Silence settled over the radio for a brief moment before Lucy's sweet voice came back. "I've informed the caller you're on the scene, McCoy."

Officer McCoy could handle it. They didn't need two officers on the scene of a woman who'd locked herself out of the house. Apparently she'd gone out for drinks with friends and forgotten to take her keys. At least she was responsible enough not to drink and drive, so that was something.

Noah turned down Pine Street and tried his best not to let his mind wander, but he failed miserably.

He'd heard about Lucy getting hit on, about some new guy asking her out after the open house. Word traveled fast in this town, especially considering Lucy's open house was only hours ago.

Maybe that's what he got for not attending, but he truly didn't think that atmosphere was for him. He was getting along just fine. The hurt was something he'd live with for the rest of his life. He just figured he'd get used to that void.

Lucy's voice came over the radio once again, this time calling him to a fender bender in the middle of the park. Chances were good that whatever he was about to encounter was more than just a fender bender. Who would be in the park at one o'clock on a Tuesday morning?

Noah soon found out there were two ladies arguing over a guy and one had ended up blocking the other car against a tree. Breaking up a catfight could be more dangerous than men throwing punches, in his opinion.

Thirty minutes later when he'd cleared the scene without incident, Noah climbed back into his patrol car and radioed the status.

"Everything all right?"

"Fine," he replied to Lucy's question.

"You didn't check in for a while," she replied.

Noah gritted his teeth. "All clear now," he told her. "Over and out."

End of conversation because he didn't want to

hear her voice right now. He didn't want to think of how that nugget of jealousy over the other guy had turned into a ball of fury that had settled low in his gut.

Honestly, Noah didn't know what had been said between Lucy and the man. And why wouldn't someone ask her out? Lucy was stunning, she was independent, she had a great career ahead of her helping so many people. She was giving, loyal and sexy as hell.

He raked a hand down his face, smarting when his palm hit his bruised jaw. What was he thinking? He needed more sleep. Maybe then he'd be thinking clearly. Because right now all he could see was Lucy with another man and he absolutely hated the image that flooded his mind.

That's precisely how he knew he was ready to try moving on. He wanted Lucy.

Did he want something more than a physical relationship and a friendship? Hell, he had no idea. All he knew was that he had an ache for her that was impossible to ignore and a jealousy that was overriding all common sense right now.

The rest of his shift went by without any excitement, which was a good thing, but the quiet made for a long night. He was slowly adjusting to working nights, though he would jump at the chance to get back on days so he could have a better schedule with Emma.

The sun beamed directly onto the blacktop as he

pulled into the station lot. He was more than ready to get home and have the next two days off. After he rested, he planned on spending some quality time with Emma, maybe have a picnic in the park or see a movie and have lunch at their favorite little diner.

When he stepped out of his patrol car, he realized he was either getting used to the weather or it was getting warmer…and considering it was inching closer to the end of fall, he knew it couldn't be the latter.

Noah passed the dispatch area and didn't see Lucy at the desk. The part-time guy who filled in as needed sat there taking a call.

He did find Lucy in the break room putting on her jacket and gathering her things. She turned to flash that megawatt smile and he wondered if that's how she'd smiled for the newcomer to her meeting.

Get over it, Noah. She's a beautiful woman and she's not going to be single forever because you can't get your head on straight.

"Everything okay?" she asked, the same way she'd asked over the radio hours ago.

Noah nodded, not trusting himself to say much else. He was too angry with himself for the jumbled-up emotions battling for prominence inside him.

Her brows drew in as she adjusted her scarf. "You've been quiet all night. What's up?"

"Nothing," he mumbled as he poured a cup of coffee to take on the road. "Just ready to head home."

He turned to get out of the tiny room.

"Did I do something to make you mad?" she asked.

Noah glanced over his shoulder and cursed beneath his breath. Damn it, he didn't want her to think she did anything wrong. Everything that he had issues with was solely on him.

"Just need to get home," he replied.

He tried to get out the back door, and succeeded, but she was right on his heels. As he reached his truck, Lucy's delicate hand settled on his arm.

"If I did something, I deserve to know," she insisted. "Look at me."

Noah spun around. "You didn't do anything, all right? I'm pissed at myself for letting the rumor mill rule my life."

"What?"

"The guy who asked you out…" Noah cursed himself once again. "Forget it. It's none of my concern if you want to go out with someone. I have no claims and I have no right to ask you not to."

Lucy stood there, her golden hair dancing around her shoulders in the wind. It almost hurt him to look at her. There was such innocence about her, but he knew she'd seen so much heartache. And he wasn't helping either of their situations.

"Forget it," he muttered. "Forget I said anything. Head on home, Lucy."

Her hold on his arm tightened. "I said no."

Noah closed his eyes and couldn't suppress the relief that swept through him. "It's not my business."

"You sure about that?" she countered, releasing him. "Because you're acting a little territorial when we haven't agreed to anything. You can't even admit you have feelings for me."

Another officer pulled into the lot just as Noah was about to grab her and show her just how much he was feeling right now.

"You don't know what you're saying," he gritted through his teeth.

"So you wouldn't care if I went out on a date with another guy?" she threw back. When he remained silent, she shook her head. "Guess not. I thought this attraction went both ways and you might actually give up the friend notion and see where we could go."

She got in her car and started the engine, not once looking his way as she pulled from the lot.

Fury bubbled within him at the way he'd handled things, not just this morning, but from the moment they'd met. It was a push-pull relationship and he was a jerk.

Damn it, he wanted her. So why was he torturing them both? The stakes weren't the same as before he was married. Now he knew full well going in exactly what to expect. They were adults who couldn't keep going on like this.

Noah turned onto Lucy's road and pulled into her driveway right behind her. As soon as she stepped from the car, she turned to face him. Her eyes were wide with surprise, but a second later, she started heading toward her back door, still ignoring him.

He hopped from his truck and mounted her steps. He managed to reach the door just before she closed it in his face.

"Will you stop for one second?" he demanded, following her inside.

"I think we've said enough." She jerked the scarf off and laid it on the kitchen island along with her purse before she turned to face him. "Unless you had something else to discuss, the topic of us is closed."

Oh, that's what she thought? Like hell. He crossed the narrow space between them and gripped her shoulders. Her body arched against his as a gasp escaped her.

"Consider the topic back open," he growled as he crushed his lips to hers.

Lucy stilled and he worried he'd pushed too far, but then her fingers threaded through his hair as she opened for him. He wrapped his arms around her waist and lifted her as he headed toward her bedroom.

"Tell me to stop if you don't want me to take you to bed," he muttered against her lips. "But I need you, Lucy. I can't keep going on like this."

Her eyes met his as she licked her lips. The subtle nod she gave was all the green light he needed.

"I want you," she murmured.

He backed her down the hall, but she put a hand on his chest as she stared up into his eyes. "Not my room."

When he wasn't in such a hurry later he'd realize just how fragile she was. The image of that picture on her nightstand mocked him, but Noah was here for physical reasons only. Nothing more would come from this because once they were out of each other's systems, they could move on.

Noah threaded his hands through her hair and backed her against the wall just outside the spare bedroom. When his mouth captured hers once again, she opened for him, arching her body and sighing into him.

Lucy's arms banded around his waist as she lined up her hips with his. Noah hadn't felt a need like this in so long, he wasn't sure how long he could hold on to his control here.

As if her thread snapped as well, Lucy reached for the front of his shirt and started frantically working his buttons loose. Pulling back from her lips, Noah pushed her hands aside and finished taking his shirt off. As soon as the uniform was on the floor, he toed off his shoes, unfastened his gun belt, and gently laid it on the floor.

Lucy immediately went for the button on his pants.

"You're wearing too many clothes," he told her, his entire body heating from anticipation.

Lucy's wide eyes met his as she bit on her lower lip. She didn't make a move to take off anything.

"Having doubts?" he asked, smoothing her hair away from her face.

She shook her head. "Just nervous."

"That makes two of us."

Noah gripped the hem of her long-sleeved tee and pulled it slowly up her body, keeping his eyes locked on hers for any sign that he needed to stop. As much as he wanted her, he wasn't about to make her more uncomfortable.

Lucy held her arms up and Noah pulled the shirt up the rest of the way. As he flung it to the side, she slipped out of her shoes and pulled her pants down, kicking them out of the way.

Standing in only her pale pink bra and panties, she set his heart beating even faster.

"You're so damn sexy."

Lucy's flash of a smile had relief spiraling through him. He picked her up and her legs wrapped around his waist as he carried her into the spare bedroom. The early-morning light cast a glow through the slit in the curtains. The beacon of sun projected directly onto the bed where he laid her and followed her down.

"I have no protection with me," he murmured against her lips. "I wasn't expecting this."

Lucy reached up, framing her face with her hands. "I'm clean and I'm on birth control. But it's your call."

"I'm clean, too." He'd had an in-depth physical before coming to SPD.

Lucy's hands slid over his shoulders and over his back. Her delicate touch spawned an even deeper desire inside him. Noah took seconds to remove the rest of his clothes and her bra and panties. When he settled back between her legs, he braced his hands on either side of her head as he stared down into her eyes. Eyes that held so much desire, so much trust.

Keeping his gaze on hers, he joined their bodies. That instant connection had him glancing away. He couldn't look into her eyes as he made love to her, couldn't allow himself to connect emotionally with her. The physical was all he could afford right now.

Lucy locked her ankles behind his back and arched against him. He risked a look back her way and noted her eyes were closed, which meant she was either in the moment or she didn't want to look too closely at him, either.

Noah pushed all speculation aside and ran his hands over the dip in her waist and up over the swell of her breasts. The slight groan that escaped her had him pumping his hips faster. Lucy gripped his biceps as she matched his pace. She felt too damn good and he didn't want this moment to end. He wanted to continue getting lost in her and never return to reality where the hurt lived.

Lucy's body tightened all around him as her short nails bit into his arms. He watched as her mouth opened wide, her eyes squeezed shut, and she twisted her head to the side as pleasure overcame her. Noah wasn't too far behind, but he didn't want to miss a second of her pleasure. He continued to watch her as his own body tightened. Only when she relaxed beneath him did he let himself go. Lucy's fingertips trailed over his chest, down over his abdomen, and back up. The pleasure he took from her overcame him and once his body came down, Noah eased to the side and gathered her into his arms.

He lay there, not quite ready for words, not ready to ruin the moment. He needed a minute to figure out what the hell had just happened, because instead of getting out of his system, Lucy Brooks had somehow wedged herself deeper into his life.

Now what was he supposed to do?

Chapter Twelve

Lucy rolled over, draping her arm across a bare, male chest. She smiled as she snuggled in closer and—

Wait. A male chest?

Her eyes flew open and everything came flooding back to her. She and Noah had… Yeah. Twice. Her body still tingled and she was sore in places she'd forgotten existed.

The bright sunshine in the room flooded through the curtains. She was used to her bedroom with the blackout curtains. She was also used to sleeping alone.

Lucy eased away from Noah and waited for the regret to settle in. There was no regret over what they'd done, but there was certainly a thin layer of guilt.

That was to be expected, right? She'd studied grief for so long, had lived with it even longer, so she knew every emotion was normal, because everyone's journey was different.

Swinging her legs over the side of the bed, Lucy tried to figure out what she'd say to him when he woke. How did they move forward? Because even before she was ever married, sex wasn't something she took lightly. She needed to have a deeper connection to someone before she went to bed with him. At this point, Lucy wasn't sure how to act with Noah. They were coworkers; they had agreed to be friends.

"I assume you're analyzing everything and trying to figure out what's next."

At the sound of his voice Lucy glanced back over her shoulder. Noah lay on his back, his hands beneath his head as he stared up at the ceiling.

"Aren't you?" she asked.

His eyes darted her way. "No. We had sex."

"Twice."

"And now we're going to be friends and go back to work."

His matter-of-fact tone sounded so cold. Why did he have to be so standoffish? That was not the man who'd touched her so lovingly hours ago.

Suddenly feeling too exposed, Lucy jerked the comforter off the bed and wrapped it around herself before she came to her feet and turned to face him. The sheet lay across his waist, exposing his chiseled abs and chest. There was nothing about Noah that didn't attract her…until now with this attitude.

"I think you need to go."

Noah sat up and raked his hands through his hair. "Don't try to get into my head, Lucy. We went into this knowing exactly what was going to happen."

True, but that didn't mean she could control how she felt.

Lucy wrapped the bulky blanket tighter around her and refused to allow that burn in her throat to turn to tears.

"I need to get in the shower," she told him. "You can lock the door behind you."

Lucy turned toward her bathroom, her heart in her throat. She just wanted to get in there before she burst into tears.

"Give me time, Lucy."

Noah's voice, full of agony, stopped her in the doorway. She gripped the frame with one hand while clutching the comforter between her breasts with the other.

"I wasn't expecting this," he went on. "Wasn't expecting you. I'm not ready."

Her heart clenched at the tortured tone of his voice. "I wasn't ready, either," she admitted. "But here we are."

Lucy shifted just enough to meet his gaze across the room. The hurt in his eyes seemed to match her own.

"You came to me," she reminded him. "You followed me home, all because you didn't like the idea of me with someone else. That should tell you that you're more ready than you thought."

Noah remained silent, his lips thinned.

"I didn't ask for you to come to my bed," she went on. "I only wanted to see where this attraction led."

"I didn't plan on being here," he told her. "I admit I was jealous. So jealous that I had to face the fact that I wanted you."

Pain squeezed her chest like a vise. "And now? You've had me. Do you feel like you've claimed me or conquered the fear you had?"

Noah jumped off the bed, crossed the room just as naked as you please, and gripped her shoulders. She twisted to try to get out of his hold, but he forced her to face him.

"I didn't claim you," he demanded. "Why do you think I left that meeting the first night I was there?"

Lucy quit struggling. "Because you didn't want to face your grief."

"That's only part of the reason," he declared, his eyes darting to her lips. "I had an instant attraction to you and it scared the hell out of me. I had to get out. Then you followed me."

He gripped her tighter as he pulled her flush with his body. "Damn it, Lucy. I'm not sorry one bit that we slept together. I just wish like hell I knew how to treat you right now."

She wanted to be angry with him for being so cold

to her, but she recognized his earlier words and actions as a defense mechanism. She could hardly blame him. They were both new to intimacy after such a tragic loss and he was standing here baring his soul to her.

"Being honest is a good start," she told him, reaching up to cup his cheek. "You don't have to pretend with me. If you need space, take it, but don't push me away and lie to me."

Noah closed his eyes and leaned his forehead against hers. "I want to leave so I can think about all of this and how fast we're moving."

"But?"

He nipped at her lips. "But I want to stay and touch you. I want to back you into that bathroom and take a shower with you."

Lucy's entire body tingled because she knew exactly what he could do to pleasure her. She opened the comforter and dropped it to a puddle at her feet.

"Follow me."

It was some warped reward system, Lucy thought. She'd completed her online final for this semester's psych class and she was so happy that it was behind her, she was actually looking forward to doing her laundry.

Granted she'd needed to do housework yesterday, but after Noah had left she'd pretty much sat in her favorite chair in the living room and stared out the window. She'd volleyed between daydreaming and analyzing. There'd been so much to take in, way too many emotional hills to climb, and she was in no better mental shape today than she was yesterday.

After scrubbing her en suite and putting her clean laundry away, Lucy still had pent-up energy she had no clue what to do with. Maybe she needed to go for a ride. She hadn't taken the time to ride for too long.

Lucy eyed her cell sitting on the end table by the love seat. Should she call Noah and invite him and Emma? Part of her wanted to reach out. The other part wanted to wait to hear from him.

What was the protocol here? She didn't want to play games, but she didn't want to push. He'd said he needed time. Honestly, so did she. But she also didn't want their relationship to lose momentum. She wanted to keep building on what they had between them because it felt so good.

She'd sworn she'd never get involved with a man who risked his life for his job ever again. And then along had come Officer Spencer. Noah was the first man to entice her in years, and ignoring such a strong ache was absolutely impossible. All she could do at this point was enjoy the ride because Noah was part of her now, no matter the red flags waving around inside her mind.

Lucy grabbed her cell and shot off a text. She kept it simple and to the point. If he answered, fine. If he didn't, that would be fine, too. As much as she wanted to see him, she also had a life to focus on. Her semester was over and she only had one more to go before she had her master's degree in psychology. Lucy figured she'd better get a start on those résumés and get them sent to potential employers.

But part of her loved the SPD and hated leaving. They'd been her family when Evan had passed. Between them and Kate and Tara, Lucy knew just how valuable a support team was in trying times.

As she headed out the back door toward the barn, she wondered who Noah's support team was. He'd left everyone he'd known back in Texas, and as lovely as it was that he and Emma were so close, Lucy knew he needed more.

Lucy readied Gunner and headed out into the field. She just wanted to ride toward the mountainside and admire the vibrant colors of fall. Autumn had always been her favorite time of year, and Stonerock, with its beautiful landscapes, showcased the season like a star. Evan had always said the same and he'd traveled all over the world. To them, Stonerock had always seemed so welcoming and relaxing.

Rocking against the saddle and the gentle trot of her horse, Lucy tipped her head back and breathed in the fresh scent of the crisp air. This perfect fall day wouldn't last. Winter would be here soon and snow would blanket the fields and mountains behind her house.

The afternoon transitioned into evening as she

tended to both horses in the barn. She brushed them, sang to them—off-key, but they didn't complain—and felt more relaxed than she had in months. Actually, she was calmer than she'd been since Evan's death.

As she shut off the barn lights and headed back toward the house, the sound of a shutting car door caught her attention. Her heart kicked up in anticipation of seeing Noah.

Instead, Tara rounded the corner of the house, holding hands with her daughter, and a sliver of disappointment coursed through Lucy. She loved seeing her friends, but all afternoon she'd been waiting on Noah to bring Emma for a riding session. Maybe he wasn't comfortable with having Emma around so much. That was understandable, but still... Lucy wanted to see him.

As Tara got closer, Lucy noticed her friend's eyes were red rimmed. Instinct had her crossing the stone path a little quicker.

"I hope you don't mind we just stopped by," Tara stated as she held on to her daughter's hand. "Marley and I were hoping we could hang here for a bit."

"Of course." Lucy bent down to Marley, who clutched her stuffed elephant. "Do you want to see the horses or go in and watch a movie?"

"A movie." Marley smiled. "Do you have ice cream?"

"You know I always have cookie dough ice cream.

Why don't you go get it from the freezer and I'll be right in to scoop it out."

Marley let go of her mother's hand and ran right up the porch steps. When the screen door slammed shut, Lucy focused back on Tara.

"What's going on?"

Tara shook her head. "I hate him. I absolutely hate Sam Bailey with everything I have in me."

Well, that didn't sound good. Lucy figured those tearstains were from rage as opposed to sadness… or an unhealthy mix of both.

"What did he do?"

Tara started pacing on the walk. She muttered under her breath, throwing her arms to the side before spinning back around. "That jackass sent me a card in the mail. A damn card with a little handwritten note like old people do."

Lucy bit the inside of her cheek to keep from smiling. Sam wanted his wife back. It was that simple. Tara kept fighting the fact, but Lucy hoped she'd realize what a great guy Sam was.

"What did he write?" Lucy asked.

Tara reached into her purse and jerked out the card that she'd shoved back into the torn envelope.

Lucy pulled the card out and opened it. The front of the card was a serene beach scene, but the inside was blank except for Sam's writing.

I still remember.

Lucy glanced back up to Tara. "This is what has you so upset?"

Tara's eyes widened. "Well, yeah. Before we were married we ran away to the beach for a weekend and didn't tell anyone what we were doing."

Lucy remembered that trip. Tara had been so in love and giddy.

"So why does this make you so mad?"

Tara ripped the card from Lucy's hand. "Because he's making things more difficult than they need to be. We're divorced now and things need to stay that way."

Lucy wished she knew what had truly broken them up. Tara had insisted that they'd married too quickly and for the wrong reasons, but Sam hadn't agreed. They'd argued, they'd said some hurtful things, and in the end they'd split up. They did manage to get along in front of Marley, so that was something.

"Maybe you need some ice cream, too." Lucy looped her arm through her friend's. "Come on in and let's see what junk food we can find."

"I'd rather have a drink at Gallagher's and dance," she muttered.

Lucy mounted the steps and held the door open for Tara. "Well, right now we're going to binge watch some kid shows and eat ice cream out of the carton."

While Tara and Marley were getting spoons and taking the ice cream to the living room, Lucy checked her phone, which had been charging in the kitchen.

She'd missed three texts from Noah, so apparently he wasn't ignoring her completely. Lucy opened the messages and was in the middle of reading them when she realized Tara was looking over her shoulder.

"So, getting closer with the new officer, are you?" Tara asked, raising her brows. "I'd much rather hear all about this development than discuss my messed-up life."

"Your life isn't messed up," Lucy stated as she clicked her phone off. "And Noah and I aren't developing."

Well, that was a blatant lie, but Lucy wasn't ready to share just how far she and Noah had gone. She wasn't ready to comprehend it all herself, let alone be analyzed by anyone else.

"From the looks of those messages I'd say you are," Tara retorted. "I saw something about his daughter. Are you sure you guys aren't getting all cozy together?"

One side of Lucy wanted to jump at this chance to potentially find happiness again. On the other hand, there was that fear and guilt that seemed to be more present now than it had been in months.

"He brought Emma out to see the horses the other day," Lucy admitted. "I simply asked if she'd like to come out and ride another time. I was heading out anyway, but apparently they were busy at a birthday party for one of her friends at the babysitters."

Tara's lips quirked as the television from the living room blared with some cartoon's explosion. "You know an awful lot about Noah and his life for someone who isn't getting closer."

The back screen door opened and slammed shut. "He's such a jerk," Kate declared as she walked into the kitchen and headed straight to the fridge.

Tara raised her brows at Lucy in an unspoken question, but Lucy shrugged.

"Problem?" Lucy asked Kate's back as her friend shifted through the shelves of food.

"Gray Gallagher can go to hell."

"Watch the language," Tara warned. "Marley is in the living room."

Kate threw a glance over her shoulder. "Sorry about that. He just pushes my buttons and infuriates me."

"We've already got the cookie dough ice cream out," Tara supplied. "We can grab an extra spoon."

Kate shut the refrigerator doors. "What are you upset about?" she asked Tara.

Tara shrugged. "A man. What else? But I was in the process of getting Lucy to spill her secrets about her and her officer when you barged in."

Kate's eyes widened as she took a seat on the stool. "That's better than any ice cream. Let's hear it."

Lucy groaned and closed the back door. "There's nothing to tell."

"Except that she's had Emma and Noah over to

see the horses," Tara added. "And he sent her three texts while she was outside."

"Really?" Kate drew the word out. "That sounds like progress. And we know he's a hero, between rescuing the boy in the creek and then stepping in to between Gray and that jerk to save the day the other night. Noah has that whole hot cowboy thing going for him, too. That accent alone is drool-worthy."

And there was nothing like hearing that accent while he whispered in her ear with their bodies joined.

"What's that face?" Kate demanded, peering closely at Lucy. "You're not sharing everything."

Lucy merely shrugged. "Not right now. Just give me time."

Those words were exactly what Noah had told her moments before he backed her into the shower and made her feel so much, too much. They both needed time, but they were in this together and they'd have to take this slowly. Lucy only prayed no one ended up hurt on the other side.

Chapter Thirteen

"Ma'am, I'd recommend not blocking the fire hydrant next time."

Noah hated giving the elderly lady a ticket, but she'd parked illegally and apparently the shop owner on the corner had warned her several times he'd call the police.

"There are no handicap spots on this street," she argued.

Noah pulled in a deep breath and glanced around. There were no designated spots, but that didn't justify breaking the law. He'd talk to the captain about the parking, but for now, Noah had to do his job.

"You're new in town," the elderly woman said. "Maybe you don't know who I am."

His pity for her instantly evaporated. Here he was, his shift over, yet he stood on the sidewalk arguing with a woman who thought she could throw her name around.

"No, I'm not sure who you are, ma'am," he informed her, shifting his stance and crossing his arms over his chest. "But I do know that nobody is above the law and Mr. Harris would like for you to not block the front of his store."

Noah had worked four hours overtime to help the captain out while he was short-staffed today. The wife of one of the other officers had gone into labor so Noah and the evening officer were splitting the extra shift. Which was how Noah found himself dealing with more traffic violations than usual.

"My husband is the retired mayor of Stonerock," she exclaimed. "Maybe you should worry about writing tickets for actual criminals."

Noah rubbed his forehead and adjusted his hat. "Ma'am, I can't pick and choose who gets to obey the law. Please, just find another place to park and I'll see what I can do about the handicap spaces."

She tipped her chin and adjusted her purse over her shoulder before snatching the ticket from his hand. Then she spun on her heel and got into her car, pulling away from the curb and running a red light.

Noah shook his head as he walked around the corner to where he'd had to park in a legal spot. Now he could head back to the station and end his shift.

He was more than ready for a day off. His schedule had been so screwed up over the past week, he'd barely had time to see Lucy other than at work. He missed her, and that was such a telling sign that she was more to him than just a friend.

Each time her voice came over his radio, he couldn't help but flash back to when he'd spent that morning in her bed, then the afternoon in her shower.

Keeping up appearances as just coworkers was becoming increasingly difficult. She'd worked last night, but had left at her regular time while he'd still been out on patrol. When the day shift dispatcher's voice came over the radio, Noah didn't like the change. He wanted his lifeline to be Lucy.

By the time he'd gone back to the station and hopped into his truck to head home, he was more than ready to make plans. He was done with trying to dodge her and pretend they were friends who'd slept together. He'd asked for time and all this past week had done was prove just how much he wanted to be with her. At least to get to know her more, to try to understand what was happening between them.

He shot off a text, knowing she'd get it when she woke up. He needed to get home and get some rest himself before getting Emma.

As he drove down the main part of town, he spotted Gray outside the bar. There was a pickup truck backed up on the sidewalk and he and Sam were unloading something.

Noah pulled into the adjoining lot and jogged up the sidewalk. "Need a hand?"

Gray had his hands full holding up one end of a long, raw edge piece of countertop. "Your timing is perfect."

"This is one heavy counter," Sam agreed from the bed of the truck. "Another pair of hands will make this so much easier."

The three of them finally got the piece into the front door and laid it across some tables that Gray had scooted together. Noah wiped his hands on his pants and propped his hands on his hips as he glanced around the bar. In the daylight with all the lights on, the place looked quite a bit larger.

"We haven't actually met," Noah stated, holding his hand out to Sam. "I'm Noah Spencer."

"Sam Bailey," he replied, giving a firm shake of his hand. "Thanks for helping. Gray is determined to get that bar set up in the back room and he's hell-bent on us doing it."

Gray ran his hand over the new piece of gleaming countertop. "Why would I pay someone when you need the distraction and I need a job done? I give you free beer, so quit complaining."

"You just getting off your shift?" Sam asked Noah.

Noah nodded, stifling a yawn. "Worked overtime this morning and I was headed home when I saw you guys. I can help if you need something."

Gray shook his head. "No. Go on home to bed. I'm sure you're exhausted. The hard part was getting it off the truck. Sam and I can take it from here."

"I'll stop in later to see if you need anything," he promised. "I'm willing to work for free beer, too."

Gray laughed. "You get free beer for not hauling my butt in when I hit you."

Noah shook his head. "Don't think anything of it. But if you hit me again, I'll hit back and put your butt in the back of the patrol car."

"I forgot about that," Sam stated. Then he turned to Gray. "You need to cool it where Kate is concerned. That woman is nothing but trouble."

"She's the kind of trouble I want to get into," Gray claimed.

Noah was not getting involved in anybody's woman troubles, not when he had his own chaos to deal with. Now was a good time to get the hell out of here.

"You've got my cell," he told Gray. "Text me if you need anything."

Gray nodded. "Thanks, man."

Noah headed back out into the morning sunshine. He wanted to go get Emma and have a fun day; he also wanted to see Lucy. And he had the perfect plan to do both. First he needed to get some sleep.

When he saw Lucy again later, he wanted to be rested up and ready to face whatever emotions came his way. He had a feeling when he saw her in her environment outside of work, all those feelings from the other morning would come flooding back and he'd want her even more.

"This is the greatest day ever," Emma declared.

Lucy held on tight as they rode on a trotting Hawkeye. With Emma in front of her, Lucy made sure the little girl was nestled perfectly against the pommel. Emma held on to the reins and steered the mare around the field. She was absolutely a natural.

"I think you are a better rider than I am," Lucy stated.

When Noah came up beside them on Gunner, it took all of Lucy's willpower not to focus on how sexy he looked on the back of her horse. She could easily see him on a ranch. With that wide black hat, his button-down shirt with the sleeves rolled up over tanned forearms, perfectly fitted jeans, and dusty boots, the man epitomized a hunky cowboy.

And the fact he'd reached out to her and wanted to come over for a ride only made her heart skip another beat. She knew they were technically sneaking around. They'd kept up the pretense at work and had remained circumspect in public. She had to admit there was something so attractive and intriguing about keeping their relationship on the down low.

Lucy loved it even more that he'd brought Emma. His daughter was absolutely the most adorable little thing and so easy to please. Give the girl some cookies and a horse and she was happy.

"Looks like it's going to rain soon," Noah commented as he stared at the sky.

"We'll go back soon," she promised. "It's such a beautiful evening with the mountains in the distance, the smell of fall in the air. I could stay out here all night."

"Do you camp?" Emma asked, still holding tightly to the reins. "Daddy took me and Mommy once and it was fun."

"I do love camping." Lucy held on to Emma's waist and glanced over to Noah. "This is the perfect time of year, too. I love being outside, but I don't like to get too hot or too cold, especially when I'm trying to sleep."

Noah's brows rose beneath his dark hat. "I imagine if the nights got too cool you could find ways to stay warm."

That heavy-lidded look he gave her sent shivers racing through her. The blatant flirting had hope filling that void she'd thought would be hollow forever. There was a light inside her, as silly as that sounded. But Noah was coming around and she found she was, too. The guilt wasn't as strong as it had been last week. The fear was still there, but overpowering that now was a beacon of hope. Lucy opted to cling to that optimism, instead of trying to find reasons to let fear rule her life.

Between her psychology classes and her partnership in Helping Hands, Lucy had talked to many people over the past couple of years about compartmentalizing all your emotions. When there were negative feelings, they needed to be put behind anything positive. And right now, Lucy was going to cling to Noah and Emma. They were here now and they were all having a great time.

"My daddy is afraid of mice," Emma said, turning to glance up at Lucy. "That one time we went camping, a mouse got in our tent. Mom screamed, I screamed, and Dad ran out of the tent."

Lucy laughed as she shifted her focus to Noah. "Is that so? A little mouse had you running for your life?"

He simply shrugged. "We all have our fears," he told her. "Those little things move so fast. I'm man enough to admit they creep me out."

"Well, if it helps, I'm terrified of spiders," Lucy confessed. "Anything with that many legs has to be created by the devil."

"You know what I don't like?" Emma asked. "Bees. I got stung once and then Daddy found out I was 'lergic. It scared me when he had to take me to the hospital."

"Scared me, too, Sweet Pea."

"That would be a good reason to not like bees," Lucy agreed. "When did you get stung?"

"Right before we moved here," Emma said. "My

arm got puffy and red and then I couldn't breathe very well."

"I'm pretty sure I lost a few years off my life then," Noah muttered.

Lucy couldn't imagine how terrified Noah must've been. He'd been a widower and had found out the hard way that his daughter was allergic to bee stings.

The first fat drop of rain his Lucy's nose. "Time to head back," she told them as she helped Emma guide Hawkeye back to the barn. "We might get a little wet."

By the time they reached the barn, they were all soaked. The rain was chilly and instantly cooled the evening down. She shivered as she dismounted and helped Emma down. She led the mare into the stable and Noah was right behind her with Gunner.

"You and Emma go on inside," he told her. "I'll tend to the horses."

"There's no reason for you to do that. You can take Emma on home and get dried off. I'll take care of the horses."

Noah stepped up to her, forcing Lucy to tip her head back. "Don't argue with me," he said in that low, commanding tone. "Take Emma inside and get warm. I've got this. Besides, I sort of miss this part of my life."

Lucy hadn't thought of things that way. He probably was missing working the ranch and tending the horses he'd always had. The void of his late wife wasn't the only hole in his heart.

"I'll make us some hot chocolate," she told him as she reached for Emma's hand. "How about we find some marshmallows to put on top?"

Emma nodded enthusiastically. "I want extra."

Noah laughed. "Of course you do."

Lucy picked up the toddler and hugged her tight. "Ready to race through the raindrops?"

"Ready!"

Lucy wrapped Emma tightly against her and tucked her beneath her chin as she ran toward the back porch. The rain came down in sheets now. By the time they got inside, Emma was trembling.

"Let's get you warmed up." Lucy eased the girl back and quickly realized she was crying. "Emma, what's wrong?"

"Is it going to storm?" she asked through tears and sniffling.

Lucy sat Emma on the bar top and smoothed her wet hair away from her face. "You know what, if it does, we will be just fine."

"But Daddy is still outside." She sniffed. Her big blue eyes were red with tears.

"Right now it's just raining," Lucy explained. "We need rain. Did you know that's what makes those beautiful trees change colors? It helps the grass to grow for the horses to eat, too. Rain isn't a scary thing."

"Have you been in a tornado?" Emma whispered. "It starts with rain. It's loud and scary."

Sweet Emma was terrified. Lucy wondered if she had flashbacks each time it rained, or what happened when it actually stormed. The poor child was suffering from a kind of PTSD brought on from the trauma of losing her mother. Did Noah realize his daughter suffered so?

"How about we stand at the window and watch your daddy?" Lucy suggested. "We can see him in the barn while he's brushing the horses and putting the gear away. Then you can see that he's okay."

Lucy hoisted the girl onto her hip and stood at the wide kitchen window. It was difficult to see through the heavy rain, but the light in the barn helped. Every now and then Lucy saw Noah walk from one stall to the next. She saw him nuzzling the horses, no doubt talking to them. She could almost feel the pain of his loss, how he ached to have that ranching life back again.

Torn between Noah's hurt and Emma's fear, Lucy figured this was the best place for her to be. Noah needed that time alone in the barn and Emma needed comforting. Lucy hugged the girl tighter.

"Did you used to help Daddy in your barns?" she asked, trying to focus on the animals and perhaps happier memories.

"He would let me stand on a stool and braid their manes," Emma told her as she continued looking out the window. "Sometimes I would brush their hair and put bows on the ends of their manes and tails.

Daddy also bought me this special paint and I got to paint the horses."

"Paint?" Lucy asked.

Emma smiled up at her. "It was supercool. I drew rainbows on the side of Daisy. Then we just gave her a bath and it came right off."

"I admit, I've never painted a horse before. That does sound supercool."

Emma's brows rose. "Can we paint your horses? Daddy can tell you what paint you need."

Lucy smiled and tapped Emma's cute little nose. "Of course we can. That sounds like a blast."

Lucy kept her sidetracked by discussing what design they'd be painting and how soon she could get the paint. Finally, Noah stepped in the back door and wiped the rain from his face. He slid off his jacket and hung it by the door. That simple gesture was like a punch of reality.

Noah was so comfortable here and no other man had hung a coat at the back door other than Evan. But here was Noah and Emma, infiltrating her life, and Lucy had a feeling this was all the start of something much bigger than she'd ever anticipated.

"Everything okay?" he asked as he took off his hat and hung it over his jacket.

"Just talking about painting the horses," Lucy stated, not wanting to bring up the bad memories for Emma again. She'd discuss that with Noah later. "We didn't get the hot chocolate started yet."

Noah waved a hand to dismiss the thought. "We can head home. You've hosted us long enough."

"It's no trouble at all," she assured him, not ready for him to leave. "Since my nights have freed up from school for a while, I could use the company."

Noah flashed her a smile. "We'd love to stay, then."

"Let me get you guys some towels."

Lucy sat Emma down and went to her bathroom. This was all so... Well, it was everything she'd dreamed of at one time. The family setting seemed all so real this evening. Lucy planned on making hot chocolate and perhaps they'd settle in to watch a movie and wait for the rain to pass.

When Lucy came out of the bathroom, Noah stepped into her bedroom. "Where's Emma?"

"I put her in the spare bath to dry off," he told her. "What happened when I was outside? Was it the rain?"

Clutching the towels to her chest, Lucy nodded. "She was worried you were still out there, but we talked and I steered the conversation elsewhere."

Noah reached for a towel and started drying off his hair, his face, and his neck. "I didn't think we'd have too much of a problem here. Storms in Texas are so common. That was another reason I moved away from that part of the country."

Lucy pulled her hair over her shoulder and squeezed the water into her own hand towel. "Anytime you're missing your ranch, you can come see the horses."

Noah's lips kicked up. He was so sexy with that stubble along his jawline and those dark eyes. The more time she spent with him, the more she realized she was falling headfirst in love with him.

Now what was she going to do? He wasn't looking for a serious relationship, and neither was she. And she'd promised herself never to get involved with a man who had a risky career.

Why did this have to be the man she fell for? It was almost like she'd ignored every single red flag waving around in her head and pushed right on forward where Noah was concerned.

But she hadn't just fallen for *him*. No, Lucy had gone and tumbled headfirst in love with a blue-eyed little girl with cockeyed pigtails.

Emma chose that moment to walk into the bedroom. "Can we still have hot chocolate?" she asked Lucy.

Lucy took the towel from Noah and tossed them both into the hamper just inside the bathroom door. "Of course we can. I say we snuggle up on the couch with hot chocolate, blankets, and whatever movie you want."

Emma let out a scream of excitement and gave Lucy a fist bump. Then she turned and ran back down the hall.

"Are you sure you don't mind us just bursting in here?"

Lucy turned her attention to Noah. "I want you

both here. I love having you guys around and I'm more than ready for a relaxing evening."

Noah took a step forward, reaching up to frame her face with his hands. "How did this happen?"

"I cracked that wall you had up."

Noah nipped at her lips. "I can't promise you anything."

Lucy's heart ached for the fear he clung to. She'd taken a huge risk and opened her heart to him. Now she only hoped he would take the leap of faith, as well.

"I'm not asking for promises," she told him, taking hold of his wrists and looking into his eyes. "I'm asking for possibilities."

"I'm doing what I can."

Lucy took a step back. "That's a great start."

Leaving him in her room, Lucy headed down the hallway. As much as she wanted to explore this conversation even further, she wanted him to think for himself. She wanted—no, needed—Noah to realize that he could open himself up again. That if she was also taking a risk, maybe they should be taking it together…and perhaps happiness could be waiting for them both.

Chapter Fourteen

Over the next two weeks, the fall air turned colder. Noah still wasn't used to this climate, but he was getting more used to the town. The people of Stonerock still considered him an outsider and a transplant, but they were welcoming and only mentioned his accent a few times a day now.

There was an opening on the day shift and he was hoping to slide into that if Captain St. John didn't give someone with seniority the position. Going back on days would be so amazing with Emma, especially when she started school next fall. Hopefully in that year's time, they'd fall into a more consistent pattern.

Of course, Lucy was almost done with schooling and in a few months she wouldn't even be at the station house anymore. As excited as he was for her, he also hated not having her on the other end of his radio.

Each night since the heavy rains, he'd seen Lucy on a personal basis. They'd fallen into an easy pattern and he'd been at her house every evening. She and Emma worked on dinner and he tended to the horses. He'd be lying if he didn't admit the horses weren't the only reason he came by.

Lucy had gotten to him. She'd shown him how easy it was to let go and open up. He hadn't realized just how easy it was to let someone else in, all while getting over such a tragic loss. Perhaps because Lucy got him. She didn't try to tell him she was sorry for his loss; she didn't try to dance around the topic. She forced him to talk about it, to keep his late wife's memory alive.

The fact that she wasn't jealous of his late wife, that she wasn't trying to replace her, was quite possibly the greatest part of this whole process. Noah wanted to be happy again; he wanted to move on and not feel like he was making a mistake. And he truly didn't believe Lucy was a mistake. He was falling for her. Each night when he left her house, he looked forward to coming back tomorrow.

Tonight, though, Emma's sitter was having a sleepover at her house. The lady was having all of her "kids" for a slumber party where they would have movies and popcorn and games. Apparently Emma's sitter did this quite often and the kids absolutely loved it. So did the parents.

Noah hadn't told Lucy about this. He wanted to surprise her by coming alone. She'd said she was going to let Emma decide the cuisine for the night once they arrived. But Noah had already stopped at the diner on the edge of town and bought Lucy's favorite dish. He only knew it was her favorite because he asked Kate. He figured that was crossing some line, but he didn't care. He wanted to show Lucy how much she'd come to mean to him and he wanted her to know she didn't always have to do everything for others. She needed to be pampered, too.

Noah pulled around to the back of her house. He always kept his truck out of sight from anyone passing on the road. Not that he was ashamed or embarrassed, but they had agreed to keep things between them and he wanted to be respectful to her.

He grabbed the sacks from the front seat and as he stepped from the truck, Lucy came out onto the back porch. This evening she wore a simple navy dress with long sleeves and a pair of cowgirl boots. The boots she'd often paired with her jeans when she'd been in the barn, but he hadn't seen her in a dress before. And he liked it.

As he headed up the stone path toward the steps, Lucy glanced back to the truck. "Where's Emma?"

"It's just us tonight." He held up the sacks. "With

some beef and noodles, potatoes, and rolls. I decided you needed a break."

Her bright eyes widened. "Is that so? Then I guess now is a good time to tell you that I already made dessert."

Noah leaned in and slid his mouth over hers. He never tired of her touch, her taste, and he wondered if he ever would.

"Maybe I already had plans for dessert," he murmured against her lips.

She trembled against him then eased back. "Did you come here to seduce me, Officer?"

Noah's body stirred at her sultry question. "Darlin', you've been seducing me since I stepped foot into your meeting over a month ago."

She took the bags from his hands and headed into the kitchen. The sway of her hips beneath that dress had him fantasizing all sorts of delicious scenarios... none that had anything to do with the takeout he'd just brought.

Noah followed her inside and the second she set the bags on the counter, he took hold of her shoulders and spun her around. He swallowed her gasp of surprise as his mouth descended onto hers. Her fingers curled over his shoulders. He hadn't even bothered taking off his jacket. He'd taken one look at her and knew he couldn't wait to have her. It had been too long since he'd been able to touch her the way he'd wanted, the way he desired. They'd been playing it safe for the sake of Emma, and not to confuse her, but he was done being safe for the night.

"Dinner can wait," he declared as he lifted her against him.

Wrapping his arms tight around her waist, he headed for the hall.

"The spare room."

Now was not the time to question her reasoning for deterring him to the guest room once again. He wanted her now and from the way she was panting against his ear and kissing his jawline, she was just as eager. Later he would ask his questions. Right now, he had more pressing issues.

"You're so damn sexy with this dress and these boots."

Lucy's fingers threaded through his hair. "I wanted to look pretty for you."

Easing back so he could look her in the eyes, he said, "You're always pretty, Lucy. You don't even have to try."

He covered her lips once again as he tugged up the hem of her dress. Noah filled his hands with her backside and lifted her off the floor, aligning their hips.

Lucy's boots clattered to the floor as Noah trailed his lips across her jaw and down her neck. Her head tipped back giving him better access. She was all-consuming. The need to touch her everywhere all at once absolutely controlled him.

Noah lay her down on the bed, never taking his eyes off of her as he stripped his clothes. Her dress, bunched around her waist, gave him a tantalizing view of her simple white panties. Once he was bare, Noah gripped the edge of her underwear and pulled them down her legs, tossing the unwanted garment to the side.

When she started to sit up to take her dress off, Noah reached for her hands and secured her wrists in his grip. He held her arms up above her head.

"I need you now," he told her as he settled between her legs. "I'll undress you later."

Her eyes flared with desire as he joined their bodies. With Lucy wrapped all around him, Noah knew he wasn't going anywhere tonight. He wanted to stay in her bed; he wanted to be here with her in the morning. He wanted to make love to her again and again.

"Noah, I—"

Caught up in the moment, he captured her mouth with his, not ready to hear the words that she was about to say. He wasn't positive, but he thought he'd seen something more than desire in her eyes. He'd seen so much of her heart when she looked up at him. And he wasn't prepared for it, not now when his body was surging toward an earth-shattering climax.

As he surged into her again, he felt her body tighten beneath his as she arched against him. Her lips tore away from his and she cried out a throaty moan as she came. Noah held her tight as his own release hit. He kept his hold on her hips as the trembling consumed him. Lucy whispered something, but he couldn't make it out.

Once his body calmed, he pulled her close and kissed the top of her head. He wanted some answers from her. If she wanted to move forward, then he deserved some of that honesty. He deserved some of that openness she always wanted from him.

"I'm getting hungry." Lucy slid her fingertips over Noah's bare chest and down to his taut abs. "We might have to heat up dinner."

"Or we could eat it cold in bed," Noah said as he pulled her closer to his side.

"That would be fine, too." Pressing her palm to his chest, she rose up and looked down at him. "Why don't I go get it and you wait here?"

He looked at her as if he wanted to say something, but finally nodded. "Sounds good."

Lucy came to her feet and smoothed her dress down. She stepped over her underwear and boots, bypassed his clothes and headed to the kitchen, where the bags had been forgotten for a time. Her entire body still hummed. That thought was so ridiculous, but it was an accurate statement.

She pulled the boxes from the bag and sat them all out on her kitchen island. Even though everything was no doubt cold, the scents were amazing.

She figured she'd just take the boxes and some plastic forks and napkins. No need to waste plates. She had some bottles of water she'd bring in, too. A bed picnic sounded so sexy and it was something she'd never done before.

Lucy pulled a tray off the top of her fridge and stacked up all the things on there. She'd get the dessert later…probably much later.

Humming, she headed down the hall, but when she turned the corner to the spare room, Noah wasn't in there. Perhaps he went to the bathroom. She set the tray on the rumpled bed, smiling at the memories they'd created there.

She'd been so afraid at first. Afraid of her feelings, afraid of moving ahead with those emotions she didn't want. But now that she was with Noah, she'd fallen for him. She'd fallen for Emma, too, and she'd be lying if she didn't admit that she wanted that family. She wanted it here on her little ranch. She wanted more than she ever thought she'd dream of again.

For the first time in two years she had hope and she was ready to take this risk and admit her feelings to Noah. She'd started to when they were in bed together, which wasn't the best timing, but the moment had overwhelmed her and the words were on her lips before she could stop them.

Noah had stopped them. He'd kissed her as if he'd known what was going through her mind. Still, he deserved to know where she stood. He didn't need to reciprocate her feelings, but she had to tell him.

"Lucy."

Noah called her name and Lucy stepped into the hall. She went to the end where her room was and found him sitting on the edge of the bed. He'd put on his jeans, leaving them unfastened, and wore nothing else.

"What are you doing in here?" she asked, standing in the doorway.

He met her gaze from across the room. "You never bring me in here."

Lucy gripped the door frame and swallowed. What could she say? She'd never had another man in her bedroom other than her husband. After he'd passed, she'd sold their bedroom furniture and replaced it. She simply hadn't been able to sleep in the same bed they'd shared, not when she was alone.

"Lucy." Noah came to his feet. "I get loss. Believe me, it's hell at times. But you show me all these ways you're ready to move on, and yet we've never made love on your bed."

Noah kept his distance, but the pain in his eyes staring back at her might as well be a knife twisting in her heart.

Made love.

The fact he used that term had Lucy wanting to step forward, but...she couldn't.

"As long as you keep me from this room, can you

keep your past and your present in separate compartments in your heart?" he went on, hurt lacing his voice. "You wanted me to take a chance. I *did* take a chance, but if you're keeping me at a distance, we can't move forward."

Lucy let go of the door and stepped inside. "I'm not keeping you at a distance," she defended. "I've slept with you, Noah. I haven't let another man get that close to me in two years."

Noah ran a hand down his face and glanced up to the ceiling as he blew out a breath. "You trust me with your body," he told her as he brought his dark eyes back to hers. "You look at me like you want more and I can't deny that I'm starting to want more. That scares the hell out of me, because if you can't trust me in here," he said, holding his arms wide to encompass the bedroom, "then you can't trust me to form a relationship."

Tears pricked her eyes as she wrapped her arms around her midsection. The hurt seeping inside her had her shaking her head in denial.

"I do trust you," she cried. "You know I've never been this open with anyone."

Noah nodded. "I do know that," he agreed, his tone soft, heartbreaking. "I also know as long as that picture stays by your bed, nobody else will be allowed in this room, much less in your heart."

Lucy wanted to say something, to defend herself, but he was right. She honestly hadn't pushed too far into her feelings before now to see that she was indeed clinging to just a fraction of what her life was in an attempt to stay afloat emotionally.

"You've been too busy working on other people," he added. "Maybe you need to start taking care of yourself."

"I take care of myself."

Even to her own ears, the argument sounded feeble.

Noah stepped toward her, gripped her shoulders and forced her to tip her head back to look at him. "No, you haven't. I care for you, Lucy. I care more than I wanted to. You made me want things I never thought I would want again."

Lucy's heart clenched. "Why does this sound like the end?"

"We can't move forward," he stated, framing her face with his hands. "You may want to, but are you ready for me to sleep in here? Are you ready to take this public and try a real relationship?"

She was…wasn't she?

"Wait, you were the one who wanted to keep this discreet," she countered. "Why are you asking me?"

"Because you haven't dated in two years. Because you won't get in that bed with me." He kissed her softly, quickly. "And because I'm more ready than you are and I didn't think that was possible."

He let her go and took a step back. "When you're ready, let me know."

Noah maneuvered around her, leaving her to stare at the perfectly made bed and the photo on her night-stand. She was so happy in that picture. She'd had it all once—so had Noah. She'd had hopes and dreams, until they were all taken away from her.

Lucy crossed the room and sank down on the edge of the bed. She gripped the post and rested her head against it as she heard Noah in the other room. Moments later she heard her back door open and close. That final click resounded through the house. Lucy closed her eyes and bit her bottom lip, trying to keep the tears at bay.

One teardrop trailed down her cheek and she didn't even bother to swipe it away. She'd been ready for Noah to come into her life; she'd been pulling him in from day one. And all this time that she'd been trying to heal him, she hadn't recognized that she wasn't fully complete herself.

She picked up the pewter frame she'd gotten for her wedding. Evan's wide grin beamed back at her and she knew without a doubt that he would want her to put closure on her past.

Lucy's heart literally ached as she finally let the tears flow. She'd loved Evan with her whole heart. She would always love him, but she was going to have to let him go if she wanted her life back.

And Lucy was afraid she'd let the happiest part of her present life walk out the door.

Chapter Fifteen

"This isn't a sight I thought I'd see."

Noah sat on the stool next to Sam as Gray handed over two bottles of a local brew.

"I didn't plan on being here tonight," Noah confessed. "Emma is at a sleepover, though, so I don't have much else to do."

That was a total lie. He'd planned on staying in Lucy's bed all night. He'd planned on getting to know her more, opening up and explaining how much his feelings had grown. She'd shown him how it was to move on, to help others through grief. Lucy was fabulous with Emma, she was giving to him, and she was so damn sexy he ached knowing he'd never have her again.

Noah had been gone for an hour and he was already wondering if he'd made a colossal mistake. Should he have stayed and talked this out? Maybe, but knowing she didn't want him in her bed, rather than some guest bed, was hurtful. He wasn't a guest, damn it. Or maybe he was, but he thought they were so much more.

"Problems with Lucy?" Sam asked, still staring at his bottle.

"We're just friends."

A friend he could still taste on his lips. A friend who had worked her way into his heart, into his daughter's heart.

"Is that so?" Gray asked with a cocky side grin. "She just walked in with Tara and Kate."

Noah jerked his head over his shoulder, and Gray's laughter mocked him. Lucy was nowhere in sight, and neither were her friends.

"That's what I thought," Gray said, leaning over and resting his forearms on the bar. "So what's the deal?"

Noah turned back on his stool and reached for his beer. He took a hearty drink, welcoming the wheat flavor and the spices on the back end.

"We attempted more, but that didn't work out," he admitted. "That's all."

"That's all." Sam let out a low laugh. "Nothing with women is ever that simple. Even after a year apart, Tara and I still aren't simple and, according to the courts, we should be because it's over."

Noah had honestly never seen a man so devastated. "Well, Lucy and I have only known each other a short time. We just had a whirlwind…relationship. Now it's over."

"Relationship," Gray repeated. "Whatever you call it, you look like hell."

Noah picked up his bottle and did a mock salute. "Ironically, I feel like hell."

The two men tapped their beer bottles to his, then took a swallow. Before any of them could say anything, Gray got called away to a group of females at the other end of the bar. To Noah, they seemed flirty, and he already knew Gray had just enough charm to appease the group of giggling girls. From the looks of them, he surmised they were celebrating a twenty-first birthday.

Noah turned his attention back to Sam. "How long were you married?"

"Not long." Sam started to peel the label from the bottle. "A couple of years. We married right before Marley was born, which was a mistake. Marrying because of a baby is never the solution."

Noah wouldn't know. He'd fallen in love, married, then had a baby. But he would never knock someone else's life choices. Whatever worked for them.

"Not to pry, but have you told her how you feel?"

Sam laughed. "She's aware. We got married too soon, weren't really in love…at least that's what she says. I was—I am—in love with her."

Noah's heart clenched. He couldn't deny that he was feeling something rather strong for Lucy, too. Love? Hell, he wasn't sure, but what he felt was so much more than just friendship.

What should he do about it?

Did he wait on her? Did he wait around and see if she was truly ready? At what point did he move on himself?

Who the hell was he kidding? He didn't want to move on. He'd lost his wife and he'd never thought he'd crawl out from that dark hole. Then he'd met Lucy and there'd been light in his life again. The light was still there, still shining, but he was still alone.

"Fight for her."

Noah thought he heard Sam wrong. His voice was barely audible over the bass-heavy music pervading the bar.

"If you want Lucy, fight for her," Sam stated. "She's amazing. I don't know your whole story, but... Hell, who am I to give advice on relationships?"

Noah took another pull of his beer. "I lost my wife and our ranch about eight months ago. I have a four-year-old daughter. She's pretty taken with Lucy. Those two are... They're so alike and get along like they're long-lost friends. Lucy is so good with her."

"Having kids makes things so much more complicated," Sam stated. "They can also make things so clear, too."

"I can't imagine how you deal with an ex and a child." Noah finished off his beer and set the bottle on the bar. "If you want Tara back, why don't you just make her see why?"

Sam continued to toy with the label. "We're pretty complicated. I was offered a job in Nashville. Thinking about taking it and leaving Stonerock."

Noah leaned his elbows on the bar. "Does Tara know?"

"Not yet. Haven't decided what I'm doing. Marley is the major factor. I don't want to make things difficult for her, but staying here isn't good for me, either."

"I had to leave Texas, so I get where you're coming from." Noah caught Gray's attention and motioned him over for another beer. "You have to do what's best to keep moving forward."

Sam let out a laugh. "I just hang here to talk with Gray. I'm not really some sappy drunk who's lost all hope."

"Didn't think you were."

"Others do," he replied. "Not that I care. Gray is a good friend and I figure if I can hang here and give him my business, it's a win-win."

Gray slid another beer across to Noah. "You ladies done sharing life stories?"

"For now," Noah told him.

"You want to know how to get to Lucy?" Gray asked. "She's a simple person, really. Nobody has actually tried to do things for her. She's always putting herself out there for everyone else."

Noah nodded. That was the crux of the entire situation. She wanted to be the one person for everyone else, but couldn't let one person be everything for her.

"I've already figured that out," Noah replied. "Trying to get that woman to see that is like beating my head against the wall."

Gray rested his palms on the bar top. "Don't give up on her."

Noah didn't say anything. What could he say? He wasn't the one who had given up. He'd just gotten to the point where he truly wanted to try a relationship and expose his most vulnerable side and Lucy hadn't removed that steel barrier she'd had in place for the past two years.

At this point all he could do was move on with the life he'd started here with Emma. Seeing Lucy at work would hurt. Hearing her voice over the radio would be crushing. But he couldn't make her see that they could heal each other. She had to find that resolution herself.

"We have a report of an armed robbery in progress at Stonerock Bank."

He'd been right. Hearing Lucy's voice over his radio was gut-wrenching. Noah had given her a brief hello when he'd come into work; that had been the extent of their conversation. For the past week they'd been cordial, just like coworkers should be. But now they weren't even acting like coworkers. They had back-tracked to that awkward stage, almost like strangers.

They weren't strangers, though. They had been lovers. They knew each other's secrets, their fears.

Noah had to admit it. The woman had him tied up in knots. But right now, with her voice over his radio, he had a robbery to focus on.

"One report from a teller says there's only one man, but she says he's armed," Lucy went on. "She was in the bathroom when she heard him come in and demand money, so she hasn't seen a weapon. She's locked herself in and her phone is still on. I can hear the suspect, but I can't make out what he's saying."

Adrenaline pumping, Noah put on his lights and siren. If a perp was wielding a gun or any weapon, there were people in danger. Noah only hoped the perp wasn't under the influence of something, because guns and drugs made for a dangerous combo. He'd only dealt with a handful of armed robberies in Texas, but thankfully they'd all ended peacefully.

Noah pulled into the lot at the same time McCoy pulled in. This was the early bank that opened at seven to get businesses started for the day. Noah's shift only had an hour left, but he already knew this situation would take longer than sixty minutes.

"I'm on the scene," McCoy checked in through the radio.

"I'm here, too," Noah added. "The blinds are still closed."

"The teller said she thinks he forced his way in with one of the workers," Lucy informed them. "The lobby isn't open yet."

That would make sense. Get in when all of the nightly bank bags were waiting for the morning deposits.

Noah surveyed the parking lot, looking for an accomplice or a getaway car. The sun was barely on the horizon, but he didn't see any unusual cars. Just a couple parked in the employee section. Still, he scanned the street. The rest of the nearby businesses were still closed, for which he was grateful. If this robber ran out with a gun, at least the streets were still bare.

Movement in the window caught Noah's eye. "The suspect just shifted the blinds," he said in his radio. "He is holding a gun."

"I've got more units en route," Lucy informed him. "Be careful."

She'd never said those words before and Noah knew full well she was talking directly to him. He also knew McCoy and all the other units had heard her, but she'd let him know she cared. There might be hope.

Noah didn't reply. He needed to stay in this moment and make sure all those inside got out unharmed.

While McCoy called the bank hoping to get an answer, Noah kept watch on the side of the building. From this angle he could see the back and front entrances and he'd know if either of the doors opened. No movement made him nervous. That meant the gunman was still in the bank. Hopefully the suspect wouldn't catch the teller in the bathroom. They needed her eyes on the inside. She was their only lifeline between him and Lucy.

The back door eased slightly open and Noah remained behind the open door of his patrol car. His gun in hand and resting on the top of the door, he kept his eyes focused on the back. He could see McCoy get into position from the side, as well. Another unit pulled up by McCoy, instantly getting ready.

Noah knew Lucy was on the other end of that radio, but the line was completely silent. Right now, time seemed to stand still as he waited to see who had opened that door.

"Movement in the back," McCoy stated into the radio.

The door opened farther at the same time that Captain St. John pulled in beside Noah. There were several officers on the scene, but right now they were still at the mercy of the suspect.

"I've lost contact with the teller," Lucy stated.

Noah prayed whoever was on the other side of

that door was a hostage trying to escape. Just as the thought crossed his mind, he saw an arm snake around the door, then he heard shots fired…and his world went black.

Chapter Sixteen

Lucy stared at the screens ahead of her and held her breath as she listened to the radio. Gunshots were fired at the scene. Her heart stopped as she waited on the officers to check in.

"I'm sure everything is all right," Carla said as she patted Lucy's shoulder.

Lucy and the other dispatcher had worked this end of a robbery before, but Lucy had never felt more fear and helplessness than she did now. Her shift ended an hour ago. She could leave and turn it over to the day shift, but she couldn't leave. Carla wasn't leaving her, either.

Lucy gripped her hands in her lap. She willed the phone to ring from the teller; she prayed she'd hear Noah's voice over the radio. She wanted this entire situation to come to an end with Noah safe. The nerves swirling around in her stomach were so much more than she could bear.

She couldn't go through this again. She couldn't lose a man she cared about. Lucy bit on her bottom lip, willing the burn in her throat and eyes to subside. Now more than ever she needed to hold it together.

An image of Emma flashed through Lucy's mind. There was no way fate would be that cruel to steal both parents from her life.

"Officer down."

The report over the radio had Lucy gripping the mic on the desk. "Repeat," she demanded, desperately hoping she'd heard wrong.

"Officer Spencer is down. The suspect is down, too. We'll need two squads on the scene," Captain St. John confirmed. "All hostages are okay. We've secured the area, but will let the EMTs through."

"What's the status on Spencer?" Carla asked, reaching across the desk to hold Lucy's hand.

She was too stunned, almost sick to her stomach, to think, much less to speak.

"He's coming around," McCoy chimed in. "He hit his head. He needs to be checked out."

Hit his head? Lucy didn't know whether to be furious at how they'd scared her or relieved that he hadn't been shot.

"EMTs should be arriving on the scene in three minutes," Carla told them.

At least one of them was able to still do their job. Lucy wasn't sure she would've been able to do this on her own.

Time seemed to speed up a little more now that they knew what was going on and the situation had been resolved. Once the EMTs reached the scene and triaged the injured, Lucy got a report from the captain. The suspect was getting checked out after getting grazed on the arm with a bullet. He'd be accompanied to the hospital by two officers. More important, Noah would be fine, though he too was being transported to the hospital to get checked out.

He apparently had fired the shot that struck the suspect. When the suspect had fired back, Noah had ducked and lost his balance, hitting his head on the curb behind him.

Relief flooded her, yet she still had an overwhelming desire to see him for herself. She wanted to go to the hospital and be with him, then offer him a ride home. But she didn't know if he even wanted to see her. Earlier, before all this went down, she'd told him to be careful, but he hadn't replied. Not that it would've been professional, but she'd hoped he would've said something.

In the end, Lucy went home. She was too wound up to sleep, she had no schoolwork to do at the moment, and the meetings were already planned out for the next three weeks.

Which left her alone with her thoughts. Not a good place to be. She stripped from the clothes she'd worn to work and pulled on a pair of yoga pants and a sweatshirt. She'd end up at the barns tending to the horses in a bit. Since she'd gotten in late her stomach was growling, so she needed to grab a bite first.

As she sat on the bed and pulled on her socks, she glanced to the photo on her night table. There was nothing wrong with keeping pictures, and there was nothing wrong with having them on display. But Lucy completely saw where Noah was coming from. She understood his frustrations.

But Lucy had come to her own understanding earlier. She'd been right not to let Noah deeper into her world. When she'd been on the other end of that robbery, she had been close to a panic attack. She'd only known fear like that one other time. She couldn't go through that every day of her life. How was that any way to live?

Noah had been right to leave last week. He'd been right to walk away before they grew even closer with the bond they'd started. The sooner she could get out of working with him, the better off she'd be. Lucy needed to break free from Noah. She needed to not have that fear of loving someone all the while knowing he was risking his life every single day.

Leaving the picture where it was, Lucy headed to

the kitchen where her muck boots were waiting by the back door. Surely once she cared for the horses she'd be tired enough to fall into a mind-numbing sleep. She needed to do something to work off her energy and carry her away from her thoughts.

But every single thought circled back to Noah. Once upon a time her mind only held Evan. He was still there, but Noah occupied the space in the forefront now. That was how Lucy knew she'd moved on. Unfortunately, she'd moved on with yet another man who took risks.

Lucy stepped into the barn, the sunshine beaming in through the open ends. As she stepped up to pet Gunner, she couldn't help but smile at the thought of Emma painting her horse back in Texas.

The sound of a vehicle pulling up her driveway had Lucy stepping to the entrance to the stables. That black truck she'd become so familiar with pulled in like it had so many times before.

To see him perfectly fine as he stepped from his truck, still wearing his uniform, did so much to her. He was here, as if just a few hours ago his life hadn't been in danger. Noah may be able to live like that, but she simply couldn't.

Lucy stayed in the doorway, afraid if she got too close she'd crumble and go against the one rule she should've stuck to all along. The small white bandage stood out against the tanned skin of his face, looking like the perfect visual reminder that a man with a risky job was not for her. No matter how much her heart told her otherwise.

"Shouldn't you be home resting?" she asked when he got closer.

Noah stopped several feet away and shoved his hands in his pockets. "I should be here," he told her. "Carla said you were scared earlier."

Damn gossipy station house. That was the downfall of being like one big family. Everybody knew everything.

"I was worried, yes. My friends and coworkers were facing a gunman."

Noah started to take another step, but Lucy held her hands up. "What are you doing here, Noah?"

"I came to talk to you and you're going to listen."

Stunned at his abrupt attitude, she dropped her hands to her side.

"You don't have to admit to me that you were scared," he went on. "I was, too. It's natural when you're facing the unknown. But you know what I realized in those moments? I don't want to live without you, Lucy. I lost someone I loved and I sure as hell don't want to lose someone else."

Was he saying what she thought he was saying? Did he love her?

Of all the times for him to figure out his feelings.

Lucy's heart was torn in two. Part of her was elated he was finally admitting his emotions, but the other part, the realistic part, knew this could never be. She had too many fears, too many worries.

He closed the distance between them and slid his hands up her arms. "I know you're still afraid, Lucy, but I want to explore this with you. I want to help you get over your fear. I'm not ready to jump into marriage, but I'm definitely not letting you go so easily, either."

This amazing man who had just faced an armed robber after working a fourteen-hour shift stood before her ready to fight her battles. But her past and all of the doubts swirling around inside her head were keeping her from throwing herself into his arms. She had to guard her heart. She'd barely put the pieces back together and another hard blow would surely be too much to bear.

"I promised myself I'd never get involved with a man who constantly put his life on the line." It took everything in her to cross her arms and not reach for him. "Being on the other end of that call today…"

Lucy shook her head and turned her back to him, afraid he'd see too much in her eyes. She had to stay strong.

"Are you that afraid of getting involved again?" he asked. His shoes scuffed over the ground as he moved closer, now only inches from her back. She could feel his body heat permeating her. "You think this is easy for me? It's terrifying, but I'm stronger now than I was and I'm stronger since meeting you."

Lucy squeezed her eyes shut and dropped her head. With her arms banded around her waist, she willed the hurt and the temptation away. It would be so easy to turn and throw her arms around Noah, to lean into him and let him take her cares and burdens.

No. Actually that would be the hard part. Being dependent on a man who might involuntarily leave her would be the most difficult part.

Lucy squared her shoulders and turned. His eyes held hers. His tired eyes. He'd had a hard night, and had opted to come here first.

"You can't be serious," she told him. "You can't be ready to move on when you're still grieving. You just want me because you're comfortable with me and because the physical attraction is so strong."

Noah let out a bark of laughter. "You think I'm here fighting for you because of sex? Lucy, you drive me out of my mind. You make me see a future when I was positive there would never be another woman for me. I sure as hell never thought I'd find someone as soon as I got into town."

That bandage over his eyebrow and temple continued to mock her. Lucy reached up, brushing her fingertips just beneath the tape.

"Are you really all right? No concussion or anything?"

He reached up, gripping her hand in his as he turned his face into her palm. "Nothing is wrong with me," he assured her. "I care more about you and how scared you are than I do about a bump on my head."

Tears clogged her throat. "It could've so easily been a bullet."

Noah framed her face and kissed her forehead. "And you could die in a storm," he countered as he pulled back to look her in the eyes. "We can't live like that, Lucy. We have to push forward and grab happiness while we can. We're not guaranteed to-morrow and we're not guaranteed a second chance at love."

Lucy blinked back the tears, but one slipped down her cheek. "You love me."

Noah smiled as he wiped her tears with the pad of his thumb. "I've known it for a while, but I finally admitted it to myself. If you don't want to be with me because you don't feel the same, that's one thing, but if you're running because you're scared, I won't let you do this alone."

"I can't lose you," she whispered. "I can't go through that again."

"I don't want to deal with loss again, either," he told her as he pulled her against his chest. "But if I have a day of happiness with you, that's better than letting go of this second chance."

Lucy wrapped her arms around him and inhaled his familiar scent. "Why are you making sense? I'm trying to be practical. I'm trying to save us both heartache."

Noah eased her back and smoothed her hair from her face. "You're not saving either of us by pushing me away. The only thing that will save me is having you in my life."

Oh, that man had the absolute best response to everything. He was determined to save her when, from the start, she'd been trying to save him.

Lucy flattened her hands against his back and tipped her head to look at him. "You're worth the risk," she told him. "I've never met anyone who would be worth laying my heart on the line again. Until you."

Noah lifted her off the ground and captured her lips. The horses neighed and stomped behind her as if they were giving their blessing. Lucy opened to him, needing to feel him, needing to immerse herself in this moment, this man.

Finally, after so long of wondering if happiness did exist for her again, she'd discovered it. All of his emotions came pouring out into the kiss and Lucy knew this was a moment she'd remember forever.

"I think I should go inside and lay down for a while," he muttered against her lips as he sat her back on the ground.

"Is that right?"

"Unless you need help with the horses."

Lucy shook her head and threaded her fingers through his hair. "They're actually fine. I was just out here because I was too wound up to go to bed. I had nervous energy to burn off."

Noah slid his lips across her jaw and up to the sensitive spot behind her ear. "I have a better idea."

As he led her into the house, Lucy had a sense of relief, a peacefulness she hadn't felt in so long.

They'd reached the hallway and Noah turned to step into the guest room, but she stopped him, placing a hand on his chest. "Not in there," she told him, shaking her head. "From now on I want you in my bed. In my room."

His eyes sought hers, his brows drew in. "You're sure?"

Lucy pulled in a deep breath and nodded. "It's where you belong. Where *we* belong."

In one motion he scooped her up into his arms and kissed her, giving her just a taste of the pleasure that was to come.

"I love you, Noah," she said once she could breathe again.

"I love you, too, Lucy." Then he carried her into her bedroom.

Epilogue

"I love surprises."

Emma hopped out of his truck and raced ahead of Noah toward the barn. It had been almost a month since he and Lucy had agreed to start moving forward together as an official couple. Their coworkers in the department teased that they'd all seen it coming. Noah had, too, but he'd had to be cautious.

Since that time, Lucy, Emma and he had spent quite a bit of time together. They'd done picnics, horseback riding, dinners, movie nights, days at the park. There had been so many memories made already, Noah was ready to move their relationship to the next level and he'd already set the ball in motion.

As he stepped into the barn, he spotted Lucy at the other end guiding Hawkeye in. Emma ran up to her and gave her legs a hug.

"You guys are just in time," Lucy said, patting Emma's back. "I need you two to get Gunner out."

"Are we riding today?" Emma asked.

Lucy's wide smile seemed to light up her whole face. Noah figured he'd never get used to that anxious, giddy feeling each time he was with her. He hoped he didn't. Lucy was refreshing, she was loving, caring, she was the breath of air he needed in his life at just the right time.

"We may ride in a bit," Lucy said. "Why don't you go ahead and get him out and we'll take him out back. You can braid his mane."

Noah slid the stall door open and gripped Gunner's reins. As he pulled him out, he realized something was on the side of the horse. He looked closer, then gasped, his eyes darting back to Lucy.

"What does it say?" Emma asked.

Lucy stepped closer, pulling Hawkeye behind her.

Noah looked back to the horse, who had been painted in bright yellow letters: Will You Marry Me?

Swallowing the lump of emotions, Noah laughed as he turned to look at Lucy. "You're asking me?"

She shrugged. "I'm asking both of you."

"What does it say?" Emma cried, jumping up and down.

Noah focused on Emma. "Lucy wants to know if we'll marry her and be one family."

Emma's bright blue eyes widened. "Really?"

Lucy held out paint markers to Noah. "You can write your reply on Hawkeye."

Noah eyed the markers in her hand. The fact that Lucy bit down on her lip as if she were nervous was the most adorable thing he'd ever seen. Well, aside from this proposal.

He took the yellow marker and handed the pink one to Emma. They stepped to the other side of Hawkeye. Noah pulled the lid off and started writing. Emma was doing the same just below him.

Once they were done, Noah stepped back as hope flooded him.

Lucy moved around to the other side of Gunner and glanced down at his side. Noah had written a huge YES and Emma had made a large smiley face.

"This is the best day ever," Emma said as she looked up to Lucy.

Noah wasn't sure who was going to cry first, him or Lucy.

"You know, I was going to ask you this weekend," he told her as he reached out to take her hand. "I had Gray in on it and we had a whole romantic evening set up for us."

"With Gray?"

Noah shook his head. "Well, he was helping, but he wouldn't have been there for the main event."

Lucy's smile widened as her eyes sparkled with unshed tears. "You can still plan a surprise romantic evening."

"I plan on surprising you for the rest of my life," he told her. "Emma and I are the luckiest people right now."

Lucy bent down and picked up Emma, who still held on to her marker. "I'd say I'm the lucky one," Lucy stated as she kissed Emma's cheek.

"Does this mean I can get a new horse?" she asked her dad. "Daisy number two can have the stall on the end."

Noah laughed. "We can definitely look into getting you another Daisy."

"And we can save that stall just for her," Lucy added, giving the girl a smile.

"I love you, Lucy," Emma said as she threw her arms around Lucy's neck.

Lucy met Noah's eyes over his daughter's head. Nothing in the world was worth more than this moment. And no amount of fear or worry over the unknown would steal their happiness again. He'd make sure their lives were full of happily-ever-after.

* * * * *

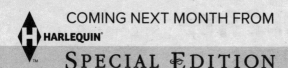

COMING NEXT MONTH FROM

HARLEQUIN

SPECIAL EDITION

Available September 19, 2017

#2575 GARRET BRAVO'S RUNAWAY BRIDE
The Bravos of Justice Creek • by Christine Rimmer
When Cami Lockwood, wedding gown and all, stumbles onto his campfire after escaping a wedding she never wanted, Garrett Bravo is determined to send the offbeat heiress on her way as soon as he possibly can. But when she decides to stay, he starts to realize his bachelor status is in danger—and he doesn't even mind.

#2576 A CONARD COUNTY COURTSHIP
Conard County: The Next Generation • by Rachel Lee
Vanessa Welling never wanted to return to Conard City, but an unsought inheritance forces her to face unwelcome memories. But Tim Dawson and his son have dealt with grief of their own and when they open their hearts to Vanessa, she's not sure she'll be able to push them away.

#2577 THE MAVERICK'S RETURN
Montana Mavericks: The Great Family Roundup
by Marie Ferrarella
Daniel Stockton fled Rust Creek after the death of his parents ten years ago. Now he's back and trying to mend fences with his siblings—and Anne Lattimore. But he's about to realize he left more than his high school sweetheart behind all those years ago...

#2578 THE COWBOY WHO GOT AWAY
Celebration, TX • by Nancy Robards Thompson
After years of travel and adventure to find themselves, champion bull rider Jude Campbell and accidental wedding planner Juliette Lowell are reunited in their hometown of Celebration. But will their new hopes and dreams once again get in the way of their chance at a life together?

#2579 DO YOU TAKE THIS BABY?
The Men of Thunder Ridge • by Wendy Warren
When Ethan Ladd becomes guardian to his nephew, he's determined to be the best father he can. There's only one catch: to ensure Cody doesn't end up in foster care, Ethan needs a wife. Luckily, local college professor Gemma Gould is head over heels for baby Cody and is willing to take on a marriage of convenience!

#2580 BIDDING ON THE BACHELOR
Saved by the Blog • by Kerri Carpenter
Recently divorced Carissa Blackwell returns to her hometown and reconnects with her first love, Jasper Dumont—can they rekindle an old flame while the ubiquitous Bayside Blogger reports their every move?

YOU CAN FIND MORE INFORMATION ON UPCOMING HARLEQUIN® TITLES, FREE EXCERPTS AND MORE AT WWW.HARLEQUIN.COM.

HSECNM0917

Get 2 Free Books,
Plus 2 Free Gifts —
just for trying the
Reader Service!

HARLEQUIN®
SPECIAL EDITION

"Munchy!" Cami cried. The mutt raced to greet her and she dipped low to meet him.

Garrett waited, giving her all the time she wanted to pet and praise his dog. When she finally looked at him again, he explained, "The bear must have whacked him a good one. When I found him, he was knocked out, but I think he's fine now."

She submitted to more doggy kisses. "Oh, you sweet boy. I'm so glad you're all right…"

When she finally stood up again, he handed over the diamond ring and that giant purse.

"Thank you, Garrett," she said very softly, slipping the ring into the pocket of the jeans she'd borrowed from him. "I seem to be saying that a lot lately, but I really do mean it every time."

"Did you want those high-heeled shoes with the red soles? I can go back and get them…" When she just shook her head, he asked, "You sure?" He eyed her bare feet. "Looks like you might need them."

"I still have your flip-flops. They're up by the Jeep. I kicked them off when I ran after Munch." For a long, sweet moment, they just grinned at each other. Then she said kind of breathlessly, "It all could have gone so terribly wrong."

"But it didn't."

She caught her lower lip between her pretty white teeth. "I was so scared."

"Hey." He brushed a hand along her arm, just to reassure her. "You're okay. And Munch is fine."

She drew in a shaky breath and then, well, somehow it just happened. She dropped the purse. When she reached out, so did he.

He pulled her into his arms and breathed in the scent of her skin, so fresh and sweet with a hint of his own soap and shampoo. He heard the wind through the trees, a bird calling far off—and Munch at their feet, happily panting.

It was a fine moment and he savored the hell out of it.

"Garrett," she whispered, like his name was her secret. And she tucked her blond head under his chin. She felt so good, so soft in all the right places. He wrapped her tighter in his arms and almost wished he would never have to let her go.

Which was crazy. He'd just met her last night, hardly knew her at all. And yesterday she'd almost married some other guy.

Don't miss
GARRETT BRAVO'S RUNAWAY BRIDE
by Christine Rimmer, available October 2017 wherever
Harlequin® Special Edition books and ebooks are sold.

www.Harlequin.com

LOVE
Harlequin
romance?

Join our Harlequin community to share your thoughts and connect with other romance readers!

Be the first to find out about promotions, news, and exclusive content!

Sign up for the Harlequin e-newsletter and download a free book from any series at **www.TryHarlequin.com**

CONNECT WITH US AT:

Harlequin.com/Community

 Facebook.com/HarlequinBooks

 Twitter.com/HarlequinBooks

 Instagram.com/HarlequinBooks

 Pinterest.com/HarlequinBooks

ReaderService.com

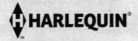

**ROMANCE WHEN
YOU NEED IT**

HSOCIAL2017

THE WORLD IS BETTER WITH

Romance

Harlequin has everything from contemporary, passionate and heartwarming to suspenseful and inspirational stories.

Whatever your mood, we have a romance just for you!

Connect with us to find your next great read, special offers and more.

Looking for more satisfying love stories
with community and family at their core?

Check out **Harlequin® Special Edition**
and **Harlequin® Western Romance** books!

New books available every month!

CONNECT WITH US AT:

Harlequin.com/Community

 Facebook.com/HarlequinBooks

 Twitter.com/HarlequinBooks

 Instagram.com/HarlequinBooks

Pinterest.com/HarlequinBooks

ReaderService.com

**ROMANCE WHEN
YOU NEED IT**